The Home School Detectives

THE MYSTERY IN
LOST CANYON

John Bibee

InterVarsity Press
Downers Grove, Illinois

InterVarsity Press® is the book-publishing division of InterVarsity Christian Fellowship®, a student movement active on campus at hundreds of universities, colleges and schools of nursing in the United States of America, and a member movement of the International Fellowship of Evangelical Students. For information about local and regional activities, write Public Relations Dept., InterVarsity Christian Fellowship, 6400 Schroeder Rd., P.O. Box 7895, Madison, WI 53707-7895.

Cover illustration: David Darrow

ISBN 0-8308-1917-7

Printed in the United States of America

Chapter One

The Tenderfoot

I was following them and I'm sure they're up to no good," Billy Renner insisted to his two friends, Josh Morgan and Carlos Brown. Josh smiled and winked at Carlos. Carlos raised a knowing eyebrow. The three young men were all sitting on the top rung of a wooden rail fence that surrounded one of the corrals at the Horseshoe Ranch. The dude ranch was located near Rocky Mountain National Park in Colorado, high in the mountains. "They were acting very suspicious. Why don't you guys believe me?"

"It's not that we don't believe you." A slight grin spread at the corners of Carlos's mouth.

"You just need more proof than somebody who 'looks' suspicious," Josh added and chuckled. "You can't accuse people just on the basis of feelings. I've done that before, and later I really regretted it."

"But it's not just a feeling," Billy replied. "I saw them

snooping around the wranglers' bunkhouse when all the wranglers were gone. I saw them come out of the bunkhouse. At least I *think* they were inside."

"Maybe they were just lost or something," Josh suggested. "Most of the guests walk around the ranch exploring the sights. It's interesting and beautiful up here. I was by the bunkhouse this morning myself."

"Yeah, and I want to explore too," Carlos said. "I want to have fun while we're in the mountains. I didn't come here to be a detective."

"I want to have fun too," Billy said. "I want to learn to ride, but I can't just pretend I didn't see what I saw. I tell you, that old couple is snooping around for something. They're at this ranch for more than a good time."

The three boys and their fathers had made the trip to the ranch as a vacation. Because it was late in the spring season, the Morgans and the Renners were able to come at a lower cost. The ranch was still nearly full. The guests came from all over the United States. Most came to ride horses, backpack and fish. Some liked to take short side trips to picturesque mountain towns. Others came to pan for gold near an old abandoned mine down the river. Stories had been told for decades of lost gold and other hidden treasures in the mountains. Over the years, several guests at the ranch had spent time searching the mountains for those legendary treasures.

The three boys were hoping to learn how to ride horses. None of them had any real experience. The boys were excited about riding the trails and camping out above the timberline near the Continental Divide at Eagle Peak. Enough of the spring snow had melted so the trip to the ranch's lodge on Eagle Peak looked like a sure thing, if the weather held up.

They hadn't been at the camp for more than a few hours before Billy began mentioning the old couple he suspected of being thieves or worse. He had even left the camp cook house that afternoon without finishing his food to follow the elderly couple. He had found his friends at the corral, watching the wranglers break a young horse. A muscular cowboy with dark curly hair was riding the bucking bronco.

"I tell you they were snooping," Billy reported. "When they saw me watching them, they looked guilty. The man smiled at me and pulled the woman away from the bunkhouse door. I know they were inside."

"It's possible they were snooping around." Josh looked away from the bucking horse. "But you're being a snoop too."

"But we're the Home School Detectives," Billy protested. "People expect us to be a little snoopy."

"No one knows about our being detectives up here." Carlos didn't take his eyes off the bucking horse.

Back in their hometown of Springdale the three boys and their sisters had the nickname of the Home School Detectives ever since they had solved a thirty-year-old robbery. After that they had solved several mysteries and had gained a reputation of being very capable detectives.

"I want to learn how to ride, not spy on old people," Josh said firmly.

"I don't think Josh really cares about being a detective," Carlos said. "He's been investigating other things, like Kim Carson."

"I have not," Josh said quickly, his face turning red.

"You mean that cowgirl over there?" Billy asked in surprise.

"I think Josh may be in love," Carlos added.

"I am not," Josh protested as he whacked Carlos on the shoulder. "I do think she's an interesting girl. She can ride really well, and I admire that."

"You also said you thought she was pretty," Carlos added. He winked at Billy.

"Only because you kept bugging me," Josh said.

"She is pretty, I guess," Billy said. "But so what?" Billy didn't understand all the fuss about some girl just because she could ride a horse.

The girl in question, Kim Carson, was on the opposite side of the corral, sitting on a chestnut stallion. She wore a white cowboy hat, blue jeans, a blue work shirt, black boots and a red neckerchief. Her dark blond hair was pulled back in a long ponytail. She sat straight and tall in the saddle. With intense concentration she studied the strong cowboy riding the bucking horse.

"She's got a really good tan," Billy commented. "I noticed her in the mess hall. She looks like she's been up here for more than one week."

"She lives up here at the ranch," Josh said. "Her grandfather works here. He's in charge of all the wranglers and the horses."

"How do you know that?" Billy asked.

"Josh has been doing some detective work of another kind, like I told you," Carlos said and laughed. "I told you he was investigating."

"I just asked a few questions," Josh replied quickly.

"Have you talked to her?" Billy asked.

"No," Josh said. "Not yet."

"I said hello to her, and she didn't act very friendly," Carlos said. "In fact, I overheard her talking to her grandfather, complaining about a guest who mistreated one of the horses last week."

"Maybe she was just in a bad mood," Josh said.

"Well, she acted kind of stuck up, if you ask me," Carlos replied. "Or maybe she got up on the wrong side of the bed. She was working at the information desk inside the lodge, giving out brochures and answering people's questions. She was anxious to leave, but her grandfather told her she had to stay another hour. She looked pretty mad. Her cheeks got all red."

"She looks really tough to me," Billy said. "I think she's taller than you, Josh. She must be older."

"She's only a little taller, but she's not older," Josh replied. "She's twelve too."

"How do you know that?" Billy asked.

"I asked one of the cooks in the mess hall," Josh said. "That young guy, Peter, the one who gives out the mashed potatoes and vegetables. He knows her."

"Oh, him." Billy looked around the corral impatiently. "When do we get to ride?"

"Right now, I think," Josh said as the big wrangler jumped off the back of the spirited young horse. He pulled the reins and led the horse out of the corral.

"All guest riders come on inside the corral and spread out," a cowboy called over a bullhorn. Josh quickly jumped off the wooden fence into the corral. Several wranglers began leading saddled horses into the corral. Most of the horses were quarter horses. The rest were a mix of saddle horses, appaloosas and palominos. Kim Carson led in a bay-colored quarter horse.

"Go ask her for that horse," Carlos said.

"I don't know." Josh stared at the horse. "It looks like a really big horse to me."

"She won't care," Billy said. "Ask her."

As the girl walked by, Billy nudged Josh in the ribs.

"I need a horse," Josh said.

The girl stopped and stared at Josh. Her clear blue eyes quickly looked him over. She did not smile.

"You ever ridden before?" the girl asked.

"Well, actually, no," Josh said.

"He rode one of those ponies at the fair back home when we were little kids," Billy said helpfully.

"A pony at the fair?" The girl's lips turned down. "Did you actually ride it, or did someone lead you around in a circle?"

"Well . . . " Josh could feel his face turning red.

"This horse is way too much horse for a tenderfoot like you." The girl walked away, leading the big horse.

"Thanks a lot, Billy," Josh said sarcastically.

"What did I do?"

"Why did you say I rode a pony at the fair?" Josh demanded. "That's little kid stuff."

"Well, it was a horse," Billy protested. "She asked if you'd ever been on a horse."

"I don't think she was very impressed." Carlos smiled.

"You haven't ridden anything besides those ponies either," Josh accused.

"Yeah, but I'm not telling it to an experienced rider like her," Carlos laughed.

"Well, I didn't bring it up." Josh glared at Billy. "Just speak for yourself from now on, okay?"

"I'm sorry," Billy said. "I was just trying to be honest."

"She must think I'm a total goof," Josh said.

"*Tenderfoot* was the word she actually used," Billy said.

"I don't need help from any of you to pick a horse." Josh

walked away from the two boys, trying to disappear in the crowd of other guests waiting to get horses. He walked toward the tall, dark-headed cowboy who had been riding the bucking bronc. He was leading a gray horse right toward Josh.

"I need a horse," Josh said hopefully.

"Try this mare." The cowboy gave a friendly smile. "Her name is Susie. My name is Colt."

"I'm not a very experienced rider," Josh said softly. "She looks awfully big." All the horses suddenly looked very big to Josh when he got close to them.

"Then Susie is the horse for you," Colt said. "She's real gentle. Just climb up there, and let her know you're the boss."

"Okay." Josh walked slowly toward the horse's left side. He raised his left leg up to the stirrup.

"That's right," Colt said reassuringly. "Make sure your foot is in the stirrup and then hop and swing your right leg over."

Josh pushed down hard and began to swing his right leg through the air. He was just about to straddle the horse when he felt his left leg slipping.

"Whoa!" Josh cried out as the stirrup and saddle and blanket slipped down the side of the horse. Josh tried to hold on, but his foot came out of the stirrup, and before he knew it he had hit the ground, landing on his back.

Josh groaned. For a moment he couldn't figure out what had happened. He was lying on his back in the dirt of the corral looking up at the very huge gray belly of the horse. The corral looked very different from that position. Between the rough legs of the horse, he could see several people staring at him. He cringed when he saw Kim Carson watching him. She looked very concerned.

"Son, are you all right?" Colt reached down quickly with

his leather-gloved hand and lifted Josh up easily.

Josh stood on shaky feet and wobbly legs. His heart pounded. He felt a bit dizzy.

"What did I do wrong?" Josh asked, shaking his head.

"Not a thing," Colt said angrily. "The saddle slipped. I'm sorry, son. Some yahoo back at the stable was careless and didn't check it. Are you sure you're okay? There's no excuse for that kind of carelessness."

"Yeah, I'm okay," Josh said. "I was falling so fast I didn't know what happened. There's a little pain in my elbow, but it's not bad."

Josh stared at the saddle that was hanging down the side of the horse instead of on her back. Billy and Carlos rode over on their horses.

"Did you fall off?" Carlos asked with a frown.

"The saddle slipped," Josh said with disgust. "It wasn't my fault."

"How did it slip?" Billy asked.

"Let me show you," the cowboy said. The three boys watched him as he quickly loosened the cinch strap and removed the saddle. He rearranged the saddle blanket and set the saddle straight on the flat of the horse's back. He reached down and tightened the strap.

"You've got to watch a horse like Susie when you put on her saddle," the cowboy said. "She's very gentle, but a little cantankerous. Sometimes a horse will take a big breath of air just to keep the saddle cinch from being pulled tight."

"When their lungs are full of air, they're wider around the middle," Carlos observed.

"That's right." The cowboy checked the cinch and pulled it tight. "Then they let out the air, and if you don't check it, the saddle is loose and can slip when you put weight on the stirrup. Like I said, a careless ranch hand back in the stable didn't check it. Dan Carson, our boss, will chew the chaps off of whoever fouled up on this. This doesn't usually happen."

"What's wrong?" a voice asked. Josh turned. Kim was standing behind him.

"Do you know who saddled Susie?" Colt asked. "This young man took a spill because she wasn't cinched tight."

"Are you sure, Colt?" Kim asked with a frown.

"He hit the ground pretty hard," Colt said.

"It kind of hurts, but I'll be okay," Josh said with a painful wince to the girl. He rubbed his elbow. "Like Colt said, some yahoo back at the stables forgot to saddle her right."

"Do you know who saddled her?" Colt asked again, looking carefully at Kim.

"Well, actually . . . I saddled Susie." The girl looked at Josh unhappily. "But I was sure I had it on right. I know all these horses. I know I did it right."

"I'll have to report this to your grandfather," Colt said. "You know the rules. You've got to be careful, Kim. We can't have the guests falling off horses because of loose saddles. What if this young fellow had been out on the trail or galloping?"

"I was careful, Colt," Kim insisted. She frowned at Josh.

"You saddled her?" Josh asked. "I didn't really mean to call you a . . . uh, . . . It's just that . . ."

Before he could finish, the girl turned and walked away. Josh felt the air snatched out of him a second time as he watched her leave.

"Put your boot in your mouth that time," Billy said with a grin.

"I didn't mean to call her names," Josh said. "How did I know she was the one who put the stupid saddle on the horse?"

"Your back is all dusty," Carlos said. Josh turned and tried to look over his shoulder. He brushed his back quickly. He tucked in his shirt.

"I didn't mean to call her a yahoo," Josh said to Colt.

"That's all right, son," Colt said. "She was careless and should know better. I've told her grandfather she's too young to be working like a regular wrangler. She's a good rider, but this is a business and she's still a kid. I hate to see her making mistakes. I won't be too hard on her, though, because she's been under a strain lately."

"Really? What kind of strain?" Josh asked.

"Don't you worry about it," Colt said evenly. "You kids are here to have fun. Now let's try this again and see if we can get you on top of the horse instead of underneath." He held the stirrup out for Josh.

Josh put his left foot up a second time. He swung his right leg over and landed in the saddle. He gripped the saddle horn with both hands. He let out a deep breath. "I finally made it up here." Josh smiled nervously. He looked over at Billy and Carlos with a new sense of pride tinged with anxiety.

"You need the reins." Colt handed the two leather straps to Josh. "Try not to drop them, and don't pull too tight."

"Gotcha." Josh pulled back on the reins. Susie immediately reared back her head and snorted loudly. The sudden response caused Josh to drop one rein. Colt reached down patiently and handed it too him.

"Sorry." Josh's face turned red.

"Don't hold them too tight, son," Colt said reassuringly. "Just hold them kind of firm. Walk around the corral until you get used to it."

Josh rode slowly around the corral, watching the other riders choose their horses. He sat up straight. Walking the horse didn't seem too hard. Billy and Carlos ambled over on their horses.

"I'm riding Samantha," Billy said proudly. "She's a real good horse."

"My horse's name is Buford," Carlos said. "What kind of name is that for a horse? That's a dumb name. I hope they give me a better horse next time. He doesn't have much energy. As soon as I got on he started walking back to the stables."

Josh stared across the corral, watching Kim help an older woman up on a horse. Billy and Carlos observed their friend's interest.

"You're not making the best of impressions on her," Carlos observed dryly.

"Yeah, calling someone a yahoo to their face isn't exactly a compliment," Billy added. "If you like her, why did you call her a name before you even knew her?"

"I didn't say I liked her," Josh insisted. "And how did I know she didn't saddle the horse right?"

"They're headed out of the gate to the big field," Carlos said. "Let's go!"

"Giddyup!" Billy turned the horse's head with the reins. His brown horse began to trot toward the gate. Carlos's horse followed Billy's, but only at a walk. Josh watched anxiously as his friends got farther away. All the other riders and horses in the corral were going out the gate into the big field.

"Let's go," Josh said to Susie. The big horse turned her head and looked at him with her big, wet right eye. Then she leaned down to nibble at something on the ground. Josh sighed.

"Come on, Josh." Billy was already at the gate.

"I'm trying!" Josh pulled the reins tighter, and the big horse snorted. "Let's go! Giddyup."

The horse continued to graze. Josh frowned. All he could see was dirt.

"There's nothing down there to eat and you know it, you stupid horse," Josh muttered in disgust. He took the reins more firmly and pulled her head up. He took a deep breath. "Now, let's go. Giddyup!"

Josh dug his heels into the horse's flanks with emphasis. Without warning the horse jumped forward. Immediately she was in a gallop. She ran for the gate so suddenly that Josh lost his balance in the saddle. Up ahead, he could see Kim watching him. He was still trying to get his balance with his feet firmly in the stirrups when he dropped the left rein.

"Whoa! Stop! Help!" Josh cried as Susie shot through the gate past Kim and the other riders.

"Where are you going, Josh?" Billy yelled out. Josh didn't try to answer. He was too busy concentrating on how to stay on the big horse. Once out in the field, the gray mare really began to run. Her ears lay back and her nostrils flared. The loose rein flapped in the breeze. Josh yelled again, trying to hold on to the runaway horse.

Chapter Two

Runaway Horse

Whoa, Susie! Whoa!" Josh yelled out as he struggled to stay on the back of the racing horse.

The ground was a blur beneath his feet as the big horse galloped through the field. Her hooves drummed the ground. The big field suddenly didn't seem so big anymore as Josh looked up and saw a distant grove of trees and a barbed-wire fence.

"Where are you going, Susie?" Josh shouted in terror. "There's no gate up there. Where are you going?"

The big horse's ears were still flat against her head. Her long strides ate up ground faster than Josh thought possible. The barbed wire got closer and closer.

"Whoa, Susie!" Josh yelled. "Please stop! I won't kick you so hard . . ."

The big horse didn't seem to hear. She headed straight for the fence. Josh gripped the saddle horn with both hands. In the process he dropped the other rein.

Josh's eyes opened wide with terror. "You aren't going to jump, are you, Susie?" The horse's hooves hit the ground in a thundering thuds. They were almost to the fence. Josh squeezed the saddle horn more tightly.

He could see branches and other debris caught in the barbs on the fence. Then suddenly, without warning, Susie jerked to a stop right before the fence. Josh lurched forward, rising up out of the saddle, leaning so far forward that his cheek brushed Susie's long neck. If he hadn't been holding the saddle horn so tightly, he would have shot right over the horse's head. As it was, the palm of his hand burned from trying to hold on.

He sat back in the saddle with a hard slap. Susie turned sideways and then stood still. She bent her head down to nibble on some grass. The wild ride was over.

Behind him Josh could hear pounding hooves. He turned. Kim Carson was riding toward him at breakneck speed, her face deep red. His heart was pounding so hard he didn't really care. He was just glad to be in one piece. He jumped off the big horse, but the front of his shirt caught on the side of the saddle, ripping away two buttons. Josh was glad to have both feet on the ground. His legs felt wobbly. He was embarrassed that he had ripped his shirt. He could see his white undershirt. He tried to pull the shirt back together as Kim rode up.

"Why on earth did you start galloping inside the corral?" Kim demanded. Her lips were pressed tight. She was angry. "You could have run over someone at that speed or hurt Susie. Are you trying to show off?"

"I wasn't trying to show off," Josh said quickly. "She wouldn't go. I just gave her a nudge with my heels. The next thing I knew, she took off so suddenly I dropped the reins. I thought she was a gentle horse."

"She is gentle," Kim said with a frown. "That doesn't mean she can't run. You have to control her."

"I tried, but I dropped the reins when she started to run." Josh hoped his face wasn't too red.

"Well, don't think about trying to blame that on me," Kim said. "I know I saddled her right."

"I'm not blaming you," Josh retorted. "I was just trying to—"

"You all right?" Colt, the handsome cowboy, called out as he rode up. He looked Josh and the horse over quickly.

"I'm fine," Josh said. "She started to run, and I dropped the reins."

"She was just showing you her stuff." Colt's tanned face was lined with pleasant wrinkles. "I didn't know ol' Susie had that much spunk in her. They must have fed her a second bowl of oats this morning and added a few wild oats."

"She can run like the wind," Josh said with new appreciation of the big horse. "She's not an old gray mare, I guess."

"No, she's not." Colt laughed at Josh's joke.

"I thought she was going to jump that fence," Josh said.

"Susie's too lazy to do that, I reckon," Colt said with his crooked grin. "But you never know. A horse can surprise you. That's why you always have to be alert when you're riding. You want to especially watch a horse's ears. If they lie back, the horse is either getting ready to kick or run."

"Do you think I need a different horse?" Josh asked anxiously. "I mean, maybe she doesn't like me or something. She's got a lot of spirit. Maybe she's too much horse for me. I'm just a beginner."

"You think Susie has a lot of spirit?" Kim asked. "She's

one of the most gentle horses out here. Maybe you should stick to riding bicycles or skateboards."

"Kim, that's enough!" Colt snapped. The cowboy's eyes got suddenly hard. The girl's cheeks got red. She acted as if she would say more, then stopped.

"I'll go back to the group." Kim gave Josh a withering look and turned her horse around. She galloped back to the group of riders near the gate.

"She must think I'm an idiot," Josh said to Colt.

"Don't worry about her," Colt said. "You just get back on Susie and walk her over to your friends. Get used to her, and let her get used to you. You'll do fine once you get the hang of it."

"Okay," Josh said. Colt waited until Josh got back in the saddle. Then the tall cowboy rode off. He galloped across the field to talk to a tall gentleman riding a fancy gray Arabian horse. He wore a flat Argentine gaucho hat instead of a western hat.

Josh nudged Susie into a walk, guiding her over to Billy and Carlos, who were still near the corral gate.

"Wow! Your horse runs really fast," Billy said with admiration. "I hope my horse goes that fast."

"Maybe you weren't meant to be a cowboy," Carlos said as Josh rode up. He tried to hide his grin. "You made another big impression on Kim Carson too."

"She must think I'm the jerk of the decade," Josh agreed. "I can't believe I dropped the stupid reins. I thought Susie would jump over that barbed-wire fence. If she hadn't stopped, I don't know what I would have done."

"That would have been great!" Billy said.

"Everyone out here probably thinks I'm some greenhorn

dope," Josh said with embarrassment. He tried to pull the front of his shirt together so his undershirt wouldn't show. "I'm just glad my dad didn't see that. You guys don't need to tell him about all this stuff. Maybe I should have gone fishing with them instead."

"No way," Carlos said. "You wanted to learn about riding horses. Now you're learning. You can always fish back in Springdale."

"Not trout fishing with flies," Josh replied.

"Don't give up, Josh," Billy said. "You'll get the hang of it. Besides, now you need to show that girl you aren't a total yahoo yourself. Even if you did pop your buttons."

"She said I should stick to riding my bicycle and skateboard," Josh grunted.

"She's kind of snobby if you ask me," Carlos replied. "I wouldn't worry about her."

"I don't care what she thinks," Josh insisted. "I couldn't care less. I'm going to learn to ride this horse."

"They're watching us," Billy whispered excitedly.

"What?"

"That old couple," Billy said. "See, over by the corral gate. They're watching us."

"I think they're watching that guy from New Mexico." Carlos looked over his shoulder. "He brought his own horse here in a horse trailer this morning. He had a brand-new pickup truck pulling the trailer. He must be really rich if he brings his own horse to the ranch."

"Probably," Carlos agreed. "I heard some of the other cowboys talking about him. They say his horse is a well-known Arabian horse. Real good quality. They said his name was Carlos too. Carlos Paloma. From New Mexico somewhere."

"He does have a nice horse," Josh observed. He looked over at the old couple who seemed to be looking at them. "I think that couple is looking at him too and not us."

Josh and his friends rode around slowly in the big field, getting to know the horses. Colt and the other cowhands called out helpful hints to the riders. Several times Josh rode through the corner of the field where Mr. Paloma was riding his Arabian. The tall man sat perfectly straight in the saddle. He seemed to be able to make the horse walk forward or backward with hardly moving the reins or using his heels. In fact, Josh couldn't see him doing anything.

"I don't get it," Josh said as Billy rode over. "That Mr. Paloma has his horse doing all sorts of neat stuff, but he doesn't do or say anything as far as I can tell."

"Maybe it's a trick horse, like one in the movies," Billy said. "Maybe he's just showing off."

"That's not it," Carlos said. "I overheard some of the cowhands talking. Mr. Paloma is an expert rider, they said. He hardly uses the reins but sort of just nudges the horse with his legs or shifts in the saddle, and the horse just knows what to do."

"I can't see how he does it." Josh shook his head. "But he's doing something right."

"I want to change my shirt before we go on the trail ride." He changed the subject. "I keep trying to keep it pulled together, and it keeps coming open. I'm going back to the cabin. You guys want to come?"

"Why not?" Carlos said. "What do we do with the horses?"

"We can just park them by the corral." Billy had already turned his horse and headed for the split-rail fence. Josh and

Carlos were close behind. While the others were still out in the field riding, the three boys tied their reins to the top rail of the fence.

They climbed through the railing and headed out across the ranch. The three boys hurried down the rock-lined trail that led to their cabin. They went inside. Josh quickly changed his shirt. He tucked it in as they went outside. They walked back down the path toward the corral. Several tall trees lined the path. Not a soul was in sight.

"Look!" Billy whispered. "I just saw that old couple sneak into that building down there."

"What?" Josh asked in disbelief. "How do you know they were sneaking? You're just imagining stuff."

"Oh yeah? Well, they went in through the side window, Josh," Billy said. "Why would they do that if they weren't sneaking?"

Josh didn't have an answer. The two boys stared at Billy and then back at the old building.

"I guess maybe we're on a case after all," Josh said finally. "Let's go take a look."

Chapter Three

Inside the Barn

The three boys walked quickly down the trail until they were about fifty feet from the building. It looked like a small barn or shed that was seldom used. The boards were old and gray. Weeds had grown up around the big sliding doors on the front of the building. A large padlock held the two big doors securely shut.

They ran up and crouched behind a hay wagon near the building. The wagon was hitched to a tractor.

"What do we do?" Billy whispered as they stared at the window.

"Let's just take a peek through the window," Josh said.

"What if they see us?" Carlos asked.

"What do we care?" Billy asked. "They're the ones sneaking through windows."

"We can peek through the other window." Josh pointed to a window on the front of the building near the sliding doors.

"Come on."

Josh stood up and walked casually up to the front window. He slowly peeked around the edge.

"What do you see?" Billy demanded in a whisper.

"I see an old Jeep and a pickup truck with a trailer parked inside," Josh said.

"Where are the couple?" Carlos asked.

"I don't see them," Josh said. "No, wait. They're up in a loft."

"What?" Billy asked.

"They're up in a hay loft, turning over bales of hay," Josh said. "That's odd. They're moving the hay around."

"Why?" Billy asked.

"How do I know?" Josh asked. "They just moved another bale."

"They're looking for something," Billy said.

"Obviously," Josh replied. "Wait. They've stopped. Uh- oh. They're coming back down the loft ladder."

Josh drew his head back. He peered around the window again.

"Let's run!" Josh said frantically. He pulled his friends back toward the tractor and hay wagon.

They hid behind a big tractor wheel. Josh peered around the huge black tire. Billy and Carlos also looked.

The back window of the old shed opened. The man helped the woman out, then he followed. He looked around to see if anyone was watching. He then closed the window. He took the woman by the arm. They walked quickly away from the shed.

"Let's follow them," Billy said.

"Only at a distance," Josh said. "For a moment, when they

were coming down the ladder, I thought he saw me looking through the window."

"They're walking straight toward the corral," Billy said with disappointment.

"They'll see us," Carlos said.

"So what?" Josh replied.

The old couple walked over to the split-rail fence near where the three boys had left their horses. They looked out at the field, watching the cowboys and ranch guests practice riding.

"They'll see us for sure now," Carlos said.

"Let's just keep going," Josh said. They walked to the corral. The old man and woman smiled when they saw the three boys. Josh smiled back.

"We got back just in time." Josh slipped through the rails on the fence. "They're lining up to go out on a trail."

"Hurry up." Carlos was the first one on his horse. Billy was the last.

"Let's go," Josh said to Billy. The younger boy looked frustrated.

"Are you sure?" Billy whispered. He looked over at the couple leaning on the fence.

"Yes," Josh said firmly. He turned Susie toward the riders lining up at the far end of the field. All the riders were lined up except the cowhands and the man on the fine Arabian horse. He was in another corner of the field, riding in small circles by himself.

"All right." Billy saw the line of riders going out a small gate.

"Come on, Susie." Josh patted the gray mare's neck. "Let's be a good girl and follow those other horses."

To his delight, Susie turned her head when he pulled the reins. Billy took the lead, followed by Carlos. Josh brought up the rear. Susie followed the other horses obediently. The three boys caught up with the line of riders when they got to the edge of the field.

As soon as they hit the trail, Billy began to spill out theories about what the old couple was doing.

"I bet they're looking for a treasure map or something," Billy said.

"They were sure looking for something," Carlos agreed.

"Then it could have been a treasure map, right?"

"I suppose."

"That's a wild guess." Josh held onto his reins carefully. Susie seemed comfortable walking on the trail.

"Then what do you think they were doing up in the loft moving hay bales?" Billy asked.

"I don't know," Josh said. "I can't make any sense out of it."

"But you have to admit it was odd that they were sneaking in through the window," Carlos said. "I think we should tell someone about it."

"Who would we tell?"

"We could tell Kim's grandfather," Carlos replied. "He's the boss around here and seems like a nice enough man."

"Yeah," Billy said. "And if we turn those thieves in, he'll be happy and tell Kim all about it, and then she'll probably like you after all."

"I don't care what she thinks," Josh insisted. But he had been keeping a constant eye on her the whole time they had been riding on the trail. She rode several horses ahead of him, talking mostly to a woman who looked sort of like Josh's mother. Every once in a while she looked back at Josh and the others behind her, making sure the other riders were doing all right. Josh kept hoping she would look at him or acknowledge him in some way, but she didn't even seem to notice him.

"She must think I'm a total idiot," Josh muttered. "I'm glad I changed my shirt."

The trail ran by the river for a while and then circled away up above a small ridge above the ranch. They rode parallel to the ridge. Being higher up gave them a beautiful view of the valley.

The ride went without incident. They went in a long circle around the camp, across the river and into a meadow. They rode through the meadow, crossed the river at a different place and returned to the camp, stopping at the stables. Josh got off Susie. Kim walked over.

"I'll take her," she said.

"She's a nice horse," Josh said.

"She's one of our best." Kim snatched the reins.

"I think your grandfather is motioning to you," Josh said.

Colt, the handsome cowboy, and an older man with a worn tan cowboy hat were talking by the office building near the stables. The old man was frowning. Josh recognized him as Dan Carson, Kim's grandfather. He was looking at Kim.

"Kim, can you come here?" the older man asked.

"I guess I won't take Susie," Kim said flatly. She handed back the reins. "Give him to Pinkey or someone." She walked slowly over to Colt and her grandfather; her eyes looked like a storm was brewing behind them.

A cowhand took the horse away from Josh. He hardly noticed because he was watching Kim. Billy and Carlos walked over, without their horses.

"I bet she's getting in trouble for that saddle slipping," Billy said.

"I guess." Josh felt sorry for Kim. "I wonder if her parents live out here."

The older man was talking sternly to Kim. Colt stood by and watched, his arms folded across his chest. Kim looked at the ground. She nodded her head a few times and then walked quickly away, back to the stables. She lifted her head for a moment and saw Josh watching her. Josh quickly looked away.

"She's in trouble," Billy said. "Serves her right for being so snotty to you."

"She wasn't so bad," Josh said.

"I want to tell Mr. Carson about that couple in the barn," Billy said. "Do you think I should?"

"I think we all should," Josh said. The older man was looking at a clipboard with reading glasses perched on the middle of his nose when the three boys walked over to him.

"What can I do for you fellas?" Mr. Carson said in his deep voice.

"I'm Josh Morgan," Josh said quickly and then introduced Billy and Carlos. The man nodded and looked back at Josh.

"Oh, so you're the young man whose saddle slipped," Mr. Carson said.

"Yes, but I'm not here to talk about that," Josh said.

"Oh?" the older man asked in surprise.

"No, sir," Josh said.

"We came to report suspicious activity, Mr. Carson," Billy piped up.

"Is that a fact?" The older man turned to Billy. "What suspicious activity are you referring to, young man?"

"We saw someone sneak in through the window of that old barn over there." Josh pointed across the way at the barn by the parked tractor.

"That's one of our utility sheds. Let's go take a look. Come with me." The man walked directly toward the shed with long strides. The boys almost had to run to keep up. He took out a big key ring when he got to the barn and opened the lock. He slid one of the big doors to the side. Light streamed into the barn.

"I've got my Jeep in here." Mr. Carson smiled and patted the hood of the old olive-green Jeep. "I call her Betty. Drove one just like her in World War II. Drove all over Europe, dodging bombs and bullets. They're the best thing on wheels if you ask me. I rescued Betty from a surplus store that was going out of business in Cheyenne about twenty years ago. She drinks more than her share of oil, but she's a sweetheart."

"You mean that old Jeep?" Billy asked.

"She's more than just a Jeep, son." Mr. Carson smiled. "She's almost like family."

"That's a really nice pickup," Carlos said. The pickup had New Mexico license plates.

"That belongs to one of our guests," Mr. Carson said. "He came from New Mexico and brought his own horse with him."

"We saw him out by the corral," Josh said. "His name is Mr. Paloma, isn't it?"

"That's him," the old man nodded. "Now, tell me what you saw going on."

"I saw them up in that loft, turning over hay bales." Josh pointed at the loft. Mr. Carson strode over to the ladder. He climbed up and poked his head in the loft. He looked around and then came back down the ladder.

"Is anything missing?" Josh asked anxiously.

"Not that I can tell," Mr. Carson said. "They didn't take a bale of hay with them when they went out the window, did they?"

"No, of course not," Josh said. Then he could see the old man was teasing him.

"Everything seems okay to me," Mr. Carson said.

"Oh," John said looking at the ground.

"Did you see them actually take anything?" the older man asked, tipping his hat back on his head.

"Not really," Billy said. "But why would they come through the window?"

"Probably because the door was locked," Mr. Carson said with another smile. "Can you tell me what they looked like?"

"They were that old couple," Josh said. "He wears a hat with fish hooks in it."

"They're right over there by the cafeteria." Billy pointed.

Everyone looked where Billy was pointing. The old couple turned at that moment and stared at the old man and the three boys inside the shed.

"Put down your arm, Billy," Josh whispered. But it was too late. The couple were looking right at them. Billy slowly put down his arm. The old man and woman spoke to each other. Then without hesitation, the man and woman walked toward them. Neither one looked very happy as they approached the old man and three boys.

Chapter Four

Corrigan's Lost Gold

I still think that old couple is up to something," Billy insisted as they came out of the mess hall after breakfast. Even though four days had passed, Billy was still suspicious of the old couple. "I don't think it's fair that Mr. Carson didn't tell us anything after we were the ones to turn them in."

"We spoke up too soon," Josh said. "We didn't have any evidence that they really did anything wrong. He said things were okay, and thank you."

"But that's all he said," Carlos replied. "He knows more than he's telling, I think."

"Yeah, they talked a long time out in front of the utility shed that first night," Billy said. "I was watching them."

"Maybe he threatened to call the police on them or gave them some kind of warning," Carlos said.

"I don't think so," Billy said. "That same night Mr. Carson was sitting with them at the mess, and they were acting real friendly."

"Who cares?" Josh moved slowly. "Are you guys as sore as me? Riding every day has made my legs ache."

"I'm still sore." Carlos nodded. The boys had ridden on trail rides around and near the camp for the first four days. At night there were fun activities and games in the big lodge. The ranch even had an indoor swimming pool. The most popular place, however, was the big hot whirlpool where the riders soaked away their soreness each night. Josh loved sitting in the hot swirling water.

That day they were all packed and ready to go on the big trail ride up to the Continental Divide. Assuming that the weather would hold, they would ride all day and spend the night up at the ranch's lodge at Eagle Peak high above the timberline. Then they would ride back down the next day.

The boys had just said goodby to their fathers, who were going on an overnight trip of their own. They were backpacking into the mountains to fish at a distant stream. They would return the next day, just about the same time as the returning riders.

"Look, I don't think that old couple is doing anything wrong, and I'm tired of hearing about it," Josh said.

"But remember how sneaky they acted that first day?" Billy asked. "Right away, that man whispered something to Mr. Carson, and then he asks us to get lost."

"He didn't say it like that," Carlos said. "He just said he would take care of it. Case closed. I think we should stop worrying about it, like Josh says. Mr. Carson is a manager at this ranch. He didn't act too worried when we told him what we saw."

"I still think they're crooks," Billy insisted. "My theory is that they invited Mr. Carson to come in on their sneaky deal. I bet they're buying him off. It happens all the time with criminals."

"That seems far-fetched," Josh said.

"No, it's not," Billy insisted. "You don't care because you're thinking of that cowgirl. I've hardly seen her since that first day."

"That's why Josh is thinking of her," Carlos said. "Absence makes the heart grow fonder. She's been around. She's just working at the desk or other places."

"Yeah," Josh said glumly. "Peter said she got in trouble, probably for my saddle slipping, and her grandfather wouldn't let her go on any of the trail rides. I tried talking to her yesterday to tell her I was sorry, but she didn't want to talk. She's still mad at me."

"It wasn't your fault the saddle slipped," Carlos replied.

"I know, but I hate to see her in trouble," Josh said.

The boys sat down on two hay bales near the front of the stable. Pinkey, one of the cowhands, came out of the office, talking to Colt Garrison. Pinkey was just the opposite of Colt. He was a short, thin man with a red face. He had a thin mustache and some hair on his chin that was trying to be a beard but wasn't really succeeding.

"That's odd." Pinkey pulled on his chin hair. "Mr. Carson is letting that old couple use his Jeep."

"Look!" Billy pointed to the utility shed. Their mouths dropped open when they saw Mr. Carson and the old couple by his prized Jeep, Betty.

"Mr. Dan never lets anyone touch that Jeep, that I remember," Pinkey replied. "He loves that Jeep more than he loves most people."

"I wouldn't lend my Jeep to any of the cowboys around here either," Colt grunted. The rugged cowboy bent down to pick up a pencil he had dropped.

"Excuse me," Billy asked Pinkey. "Did Mr. Carson know those people before this week? Are they old friends or relatives?"

"Not that I know of," Pinkey said. "Look, that old guy is holding a metal detector. He's got gold fever, you can believe that." Colt stared at the old couple, grunted and then smiled.

"Where do you suppose they're taking it?" Billy asked. "I wondered if they were maybe looking for gold too."

"Could be," Pinkey said. "Lots of people come up here looking for Corrigan's lost gold."

"Who was Corrigan?" Josh asked.

"Nothing but a legend to drive gold hungry fools crazy," Colt said. "But it's good business. It brings tourists around."

"It's more than a legend, I think," Pinkey replied.

"Foolishness," Colt countered. "Every old gold-mining area in Colorado has stories of the lost gold of some old miner or outlaw."

"Some of them have to be true," Pinkey said. "I've looked for Corrigan's gold a few times myself."

"A waste of time," Colt said. "We've got to hit the trail in about five minutes. You all be ready." He looked at the couple in the Jeep and shook his head. He walked away.

"I don't think Colt believes in Corrigan's gold," Josh said.

"He's new here this season," Pinkey replied. "He came from California last month. He's a real horseman, not just another cowboy. He's worked with horses all his life. He's worked with race horses, and he rode in the rodeo. He was champion bronc buster for years. He breaks in our new horses."

"Did he ever ride race horses?" Billy asked.

"No way," Pinkey said. "He's too big. Jockeys are real

small. They're not much bigger than you, in fact."

"Thanks a lot." Billy didn't like being considered small.

"Hold on, Sonny, I didn't mean you were short for your age," Pinkey said, seeing Billy's offense. "All I'm saying is that a jockey is not much bigger than you even as a full-grown adult. Colt is way too big to be a jockey. He just helped train the race horses."

"Do you really think Corrigan's lost gold exists?" Carlos asked.

"I think it's more than a legend," Pinkey replied. "Herbert Corrigan was a miner who had all but given up on his claim. It was off the Snakeback River. Then one day, he struck it rich. They said he hauled out almost a half million dollars in gold before the lode ran out. Unlike a lot of miners, he decided to quit when he was ahead. They say he tried to be secretive about it. He cashed in his gold for gold coins. Everyone says he hid the coins until he got ready to leave the mountains and go back east. He didn't trust the local bank to keep it safe. Back then, people robbed banks a lot more than they do now. He wanted to take it to a bank in Chicago and live it up.

"Then word got out he was leaving. He had an ex-partner named George Potter who claimed that half of the gold should have been his. They argued in a saloon the night before Corrigan was to leave town. Potter claimed he would kill Corrigan if he didn't share his gold. Later that evening, Corrigan was found dead in an alley, killed by a knife. They found Potter down the alley, dead drunk with a bloody knife in his hand. He admitted to killing Corrigan. He wouldn't say whether or not Corrigan told him where he had hidden his gold. The sheriff put him in jail. But two days later, before he could even stand trial or anything, he had a heart attack and died."

"And no one ever found Corrigan's gold?" Billy asked.

"That's what people claim," Pinkey replied.

"But someone could have found it way back then and never told anyone," Josh said. "That gold is probably long gone."

"Maybe or maybe not," Pinkey said. "But a half-million dollars of gold coins from back then would be worth who knows how much these days. Some think Corrigan buried his gold really well and that it's still hiding up in these mountains, just waiting to be discovered. His original claim was actually not far from this ranch. They call it Corrigan's Canyon."

"Really?" Billy asked. "Can we go there?"

"No way." Pinkey pulled on his chin hair. "A mining company owns the land, and they don't allow trespassing. Some people still try to go back there. An old prospector named Ben Tucker lives up there and runs people off if they come around. He carries a shotgun with him, they say."

"I bet we could find Corrigan's lost gold," Billy said excitedly. "I bet that's what that old couple is after."

"Could be," Pinkey said. "But they better not meet up with Ben Tucker, or they might get a buckshot surprise."

"Hold your horses, Billy." Josh saw the eager look in his younger friend's eyes. "We came up here to ride, not to look for gold."

"I know that," Billy said defensively. "But can you imagine finding a half-million dollars in gold coins? That would really be a piece of detective work."

"You want to be a detective?" Pinkey asked with a smile.

"We *are* detectives," Billy said firmly. "And the first day we were here we saw that same old couple who took the Jeep sneaking into that shed. They went right in the back window."

"Really?" Pinkey asked with interest. He pulled at his thin mustache. "I wonder what they were looking for."

"I don't know," Josh said. "I saw them looking around up in the hay loft. We told Mr. Carson about it, and he talked to them. But he didn't seem too concerned."

"I thought they would get in trouble, but now he's lending them his Jeep," Billy said with disappointment. "I wonder what they're up to."

"That is curious." Pinkey looked over at the shed. "You boys better get saddled up. We're heading out in a few minutes. Colt will be mad if we're late."

Chapter Five

The Three Stragglers

Josh rode Susie in a slow circle, waiting for the ride up to Eagle Peak and the Continental Divide to begin. Billy and Carlos joined him. Suddenly, Kim Carson rode out of the stable on her chestnut horse. Josh stared with surprise.

"Look who's back in the saddle," Carlos said to Josh.

"Yeah, I see," Josh replied. "I hope she's coming on the ride."

"You and that girl," Billy said with disgust. "I don't know why you care about her. Especially when she acts so snobby."

"She's not that snobby." Josh sat up straighter in his saddle as she rode by. She looked at him but didn't speak.

"See. She's just not friendly," Billy replied. "Let's go. They're going out the gate."

The ride out of camp was uneventful. Josh enjoyed it but wished they could get in open places where the horses could gallop. He had gotten over his first wild ride on Susie and, with a few more days of practice and had started to like to run the horses. But the horses just plodded along one behind the other as they went up the trail. By midmorning Josh was ready for a break. His legs didn't ache as much as they had that morning.

They stopped in a pretty meadow by a stream where the horses could drink. By that time, he and the others had stopped talking about the old couple and turned their attention to lost gold. In fact, Billy was pursuing a lost treasure himself. He was standing at the edge of the little stream, peering into the water eagerly.

"Billy, we don't have time to do this," Josh said.

"But I'm sure it's valuable silver." Billy squinted down at the water with a glimmer of greed in his ten-year-old eyes. "The streams up here are full of gold and silver."

"But everyone is leaving." Josh looked nervously over at the riders disappearing on the narrow trail up the mountain.

"It won't take long." Billy grabbed a long stick and poked down in the water toward the shiny silver object. "This could be worth a lot of money. It might even pay for our trip."

"I don't think silver looks like that." Carlos stared down at the glittering metal.

"It's worth a try," Billy said. "Come on. We can catch up."

"But Kim is motioning for us to come on." Josh pointed toward the trail. The girl on her chestnut stallion waved impatiently for the three boys to follow.

"Hurry up, Billy," Carlos said. "She doesn't look happy."

"She's just a grouch," Billy said. "She hasn't said a word to us all morning."

"Come on, Billy," Josh said.

"Maybe I can get it if I stand on that rock." Billy carefully stepped out onto a rounded rock away from shore. He then took another step onto a smaller rock. He wobbled back and forth a few seconds before getting his balance.

"I can reach it now." Slowly Billy began to bend over. He stuck his hand down carefully in the cold stream. He reached for the shiny object in the water. Just as his fingers touched it, his foot slipped. "Whoa!" Billy yelled as he toppled sideways into the cold mountain water.

"Are you all right?" Josh ran to the bank.

"Yes." Billy stood up and frowned. He raised up the shiny silver object. It was a piece of a squashed aluminum soda can.

"Is that the treasure?" Carlos asked with a grin.

"Yes," Billy replied with disappointment. His arm and leg dripped water. "This water is freezing. It went down into my boots."

"Come on out and get dried off." Josh extended his arm. "We're going to slow everyone down."

"I'm sorry," Billy said softly. "I really thought it was a treasure."

He turned to throw the can back into the stream, cocking his arm.

"Don't do that!" Kim Carson rode up. "Why didn't you guys come when I waved? Everyone is back on the trail."

"Billy thought he found a treasure." Josh smiled cynically.

"You mean that tin can?"

"Actually it's aluminum," Carlos said. "That's probably why it's so shiny in the water. Tin would probably rust and—"

"I don't care what it is," Kim interrupted. "Everyone is leaving, and you guys are playing in the water."

"I'm not playing," Billy protested. "I fell in. And I'm not hurt, in case you were wondering."

"I can see you're not hurt." Kim's eyes flashed with anger. "You need to put on dry clothes. I hope you remembered to pack your saddle roll with extra clothes like it said in the instructions."

"We all packed according to the list," Josh said quickly. "Can we wait until Billy changes his clothes?"

"I better go tell Colt." Kim looked up at the sky. Dark clouds were gathering above the western rim. She stared at Billy and shook her head. "He won't be happy about this. Don't throw that can in the water."

"I didn't put in there," Billy said defensively. "I was just going to throw it back. There are no trash cans around here to throw it in."

"When you're on the trail, you carry your trash out with you," Kim said firmly. "And if you see someone else's trash, you pick it up and carry that with you if you have room. That way we can keep the mountains clean. I need to go tell Colt what happened."

The girl on the chestnut stallion turned and rode away. Billy shook his head as he watched her go.

"What a grouch! I don't think I've seen her smile since I got here," Billy said in disgust. He put the squashed can down at his feet, then grabbed his wet pants and twisted them. Water dripped out in a steady stream.

"You need to change clothes and empty out your boots," Josh observed.

"But we could catch up if we left right now," Billy said.

"You don't want to ride in wet clothes," Carlos replied. "We can catch up."

"What if we get lost?" Billy asked.

"I don't think we'll get lost," Josh said. "You better hurry up."

Kim Carson rode back to the three young men by the side of the river. She did not look happy. "Colt agreed that he needs to change clothes before you continue the ride," Kim said. "And he's making me baby-sit you guys until we catch up with the others. I'll wait over by that tree while you change your clothes. Be quick. I want to get back with the others. Colt is giving me the responsibility to get you guys back with the other riders on the trail. I don't want to let him down and have him get mad at me again."

"Okay, okay." Billy sat down and pulled off his wet boot, pouring the water out on the ground. Then he took off his wet socks. He walked over to his horse and reached for the rolled pack attached to the rear of the saddle.

While Billy unrolled the pack to retrieve his clothes, Carlos and Josh waited under a tree. Josh watched Kim ride further downstream. She hopped off her stallion and led him to the water's edge for a drink.

"She's going to think we're all idiots." Josh shook his head.

"Well, I don't know that I'd blame her," Carlos observed.

"I wonder why she's so grouchy," Josh replied. "I don't think we could be too different than other people that come up here. After all, we're new at riding."

"Maybe we *are* different," Carlos said glumly. "Maybe the other people who come up here don't let the horses run away the first day or fall into the streams as they try to fish out trash that they think is valuable silver."

"You might be right," Josh said. "I guess I didn't want to think we could be such awful city slickers. I really thought I'd be good at riding horses. But you know what?"

"What?"

"I'm kind of scared of horses," Josh said softly. "They're

so big, and I keep thinking one will step on me or kick me. It's not how I imagined. It's not like the movies or the people on TV where they just jump on and ride."

"I think riding horses is fun," Carlos replied. "Those people on television have been riding a long time. Some of them are even trick riders and stuntmen or women. But when they first started they had to be beginners like us too."

"I guess," Josh said uncertainly. "They make it look so easy."

"It's not too hard," Carlos said, "if you do what the cowboys tells you."

"I followed instructions, and I fell off the first time I tried to get on." Josh sighed.

"But you're getting better each day. You even seemed to be enjoying yourself when we got to gallop yesterday," Carlos said.

"Hurry up, Billy."

"These wet clothes are hard to peel off," Billy shouted back. He sneezed. "We'll catch up with the others. Don't worry."

Josh shook his head. He and Carlos chatted while Billy finally got dressed. Then he had to repack the old wet clothes in the saddle roll and tie it onto the horse. When Kim saw that they were nearly ready, she rode over.

"We need to get back on the trail," Kim said flatly. "Are you ready?"

"Just about," Billy said. "Can't we just gallop and catch up?"

"You can't gallop on the trail," Kim said. "It's too rocky and steep."

"You mean we have to keep walking the horses the whole way to the camp?" Billy asked.

"Of course," Kim said. "It's not a race. That's what a trail ride is. If you want to gallop, you have to wait until we get back to camp. Now let's go. I want to show Colt I can get you guys back with the other riders in one piece."

"I'm sorry if we're causing you to have a hard time with him," Josh said slowly. Kim looked at Josh carefully without saying anything. Her face softened.

"You aren't the problem." Kim's voice was hard. "He just thinks I'm too young to handle responsibility. That's what he told my grandfather."

"Is he the reason you got grounded from riding?" Josh asked.

"My grandfather said it was my attitude," Kim said quietly. "I argued with him the day you all arrived about the saddle slipping. My grandfather doesn't allow me to talk back, so he grounded me for the week. At least he said that was his reason. I still think Colt had something to do with it. I wouldn't get to be out here at all except that we were short two wranglers who are sick with the flu back at the ranch. Now let's get a move on so we can catch up."

The four riders headed for the trail. Kim was in the lead. Josh was behind her. Billy followed Josh, and Carlos brought up the rear. They headed up the trail. Occasionally, as the trail twisted and turned up the mountain, they could catch glimpses of the other riders way above them.

Josh felt nervous riding right behind Kim. She didn't talk, though she turned around from time to time to make sure they were keeping up. At a bend on the trail, they passed a patch of lush green grass. Susie stopped and bent her head down to nibble. Kim turned around just at that moment.

"Don't let her eat now," Kim said. "You have to be firm

with a horse. Don't let her boss you around."

"I'm trying to be firm," Josh said. "But she pulls down really hard when she wants to eat grass."

At that moment, the big gray horse took a step to grab a tall lazy weed. Josh jerked her head back up. The big horse stamped her foot.

"Don't yank her like that," Kim said. "She has a bit in her mouth."

"You just said to be firm," Josh replied with exasperation. "I'm trying to be firm."

"You can pull her head up firmly without yanking," Kim responded, not trying to hide the irritation in her voice. "Be firm but gentle. How would you like it if someone had a bit in your mouth and yanked hard? You can ruin a horse's mouth by yanking."

Josh fumed, his face red with embarrassment. He gripped the reins of the large gray mare more tightly than ever, determined to keep control of the beast.

Kim clucked her tongue and reined her horse back on the trail. Josh's horse fell in behind her. The trail curved upward. As they climbed higher up the mountain, the trail became even steeper and more narrow.

"I'd hate to fall off this trail." Billy looked down to his right. "It really drops away."

"No kidding." Looking down the side of the steep mountain made Josh shift in the saddle and hold the reins tighter.

"We're way behind." Kim turned, looked at Josh and frowned. Josh looked up and noticed her staring.

"You're holding the reins too tight," she said.

"I'm trying to steer her on this trail." Josh gritted his teeth. He felt his face getting red again.

"You're riding a horse, not steering a car," the girl reprimanded loudly.

"Well, I don't want her running away or falling off the side of this mountain," Josh shot back. His face felt very hot. Anger churned in his stomach. It was bad enough to be corrected in front of his friends Billy and Carlos. But it was worse to be corrected by a girl his own age who was obviously a very good rider.

"She thinks I'm a total idiot and jerk," Josh muttered to himself as he gripped the reins more tightly. Susie stopped and shook her head.

"When you do that, she thinks you want to stop," Kim instructed impatiently.

"Why are you stopping your horse?" Billy asked. "We'll never catch up with the others if you keep stopping her."

"I'm not trying to stop her," Josh said harshly.

"You don't need to be afraid of her," Carlos called up to Josh, trying to be encouraging.

"I'm not afraid of her. I just don't want her to run off," Josh replied.

"I meant Kim, not your horse," Carlos said even more softly.

"I'm not afraid of her!" Josh whispered back angrily.

"I am," Carlos replied. "She's a tougher instructor than Mr. Walden. To be honest, I liked the other trail rides without her."

"She's not so tough," Josh countered.

"She could ride better than any of us with her hands tied behind her back and her eyes closed," Billy said. Josh loosened the reins. The big horse began plodding up the trail.

"We'll catch up with the others eventually." Kim looked over her shoulder. "There's another stopping place higher up in a meadow near Broken Wing Pass."

"It looks like it might rain," Carlos said. The blue sky was slowly being filled by gray clouds.

"I hope not," Billy said. "Then all my clothes will be wet."

"You packed your poncho, didn't you?" Josh asked.

"Of course," Billy said. "But even so, we'd still probably get wet, and my other clothes are already soaked."

"If it begins to rain, we can probably get under a tree," Kim said, looking up at the clouds. "It will make the trail more muddy and more slippery. You have to be more careful if you ride in mud."

"Do horses care about walking in the rain?" Josh asked.

"Not really." Kim's voice was friendlier. "They don't like lightning or thunder. Flame hates thunder and lightning."

"He is really a pretty horse," Josh said.

"He's a great horse," Kim said proudly. She looked at Josh. "That's the right way to hold the reins."

"Thanks." Josh sat up straighter in the saddle. A low rumble broke through the sky.

"I feel raindrops," Billy said.

"Me too," Carlos said. "Should we get out our ponchos?"

"It may be just sprinkle." Kim turned in her saddle. "Let's wait and see. I want to get beyond this bend in the trail. We'll be in the cover of more trees up ahead."

They rode toward the tight curve in the trail. A pile of large boulders made the trail very narrow. For a moment Josh looked away from the narrow trail at Kim. She rode her chestnut stallion, looking beautiful in the bright Colorado morning. As much as he didn't want to admit it, Josh got a knot in his throat looking at her. Kim slowed down right before the bend in the trail, waiting for the others to catch up.

"It's pretty narrow along here, isn't it?" Josh asked nervously.

"Yes," Kim said. "But you can bet your horse wants to stay on the trail even more than you do."

All four riders were as close together as dominoes as they reached the curve. An eerie rattling noise filled the air. Kim's stallion reared back.

"Rattlesnake!" she yelled, trying to hold on to her horse. The spooked horse whinnied and reared again, backing into Susie. Susie snorted and whinnied and stamped her feet, trying to stay on the trail as Kim's horse crowded them.

The rattlesnake lunged and so did Flame. The horse squealed and plunged down the steep mountainside. Susie, who was already spooked, saw the snake as soon as Kim and Flame left the trail. The snake struck again, and Susie followed Flame. Both horses plunged down the mountainside, their riders clinging tightly to the reins.

Chapter Six

Down the Mountain

Josh yelled as Susie headed down the mountainside. He felt sure the big horse was going to trip and roll over on him any second. Down, down, down the two riders went. Branches snapped and tore at his clothes. More than once he had to duck to keep from being knocked off the horse by a low branch. The ground was a blur beneath his feet.

The horses cried out as they plunged down the steep mountain, patches of unmelted winter snow flashing by them on either side. Susie was right on the heels of Flame, who neighed in anguish as he careened down the steep slope. The trees were thick, but fortunately there was enough room for the horses to dodge them. The horses gained momentum like rolling rocks.

"Help us, God!" Josh cried out as they plunged farther down the mountain. He had never been so scared in all his life. Each jarring step threatened to throw him from the horse's back. They seemed to go down forever. It was too steep to stop. The horses stumbled a few times, but kept their feet. Josh held his breath, too scared to scream.

Up ahead, the ground flattened for a few yards on the steep mountainside. Flame jerked to the right, barely missing an aspen tree. The horse suddenly ducked under a low branch, throwing Kim off balance. She wasn't able to duck soon enough. The branch hit her shoulder. She flew off the horse's back and hit the ground. Josh and Susie nearly rode right on top of her. At the last second, Susie turned and followed the runaway Flame. Josh gripped the saddle horn tighter.

The big horse ducked under another branch, and suddenly Josh found himself in a flat open space. Flame had stopped running and was standing off to the left watching them as they reached a flat place. Susie stopped running when she reached Flame.

Josh jumped off the horse. His legs felt like rubber as he gulped huge breaths of air. For a moment he couldn't believe he was still alive and unhurt after plunging down the side of the mountain. Then he remembered Kim.

"Kim!" he shouted. He turned and ran up the hillside.

"I'm up here!" she shouted back.

Josh clawed his way back up the steep hillside, struggling over loose rocks and soil. He went about fifty yards before he saw her, sitting up, leaning against a boulder. "Are you hurt?" Josh called out. At least he didn't see any blood.

"I don't think so," Kim said. "Luckily I landed on dirt and leaves, not on a rock."

Josh rushed to her side. He looked down at her, not sure what to do. At that moment, he realized how hard he was still breathing. He took in deep gulps of air. His chest heaved, and trickles of sweat ran down his forehead and onto his cheek.

"You look like you've been running a race," Kim said with half a smile. "Are you okay?"

"I guess," Josh said. "I've never been so scared in my life. I can't believe we rode down this mountain."

"At least you stayed on your horse," Kim grunted. She looked at him with new respect.

"I don't know how." Josh was still trying to get his breath. "I was praying the whole way down."

"I was too scared to even think. I can't believe the horses didn't fall."

"God was watching out for us."

"I wish he had watched out for me before we started down this mountain," Kim said angrily. "The last time I fell off my horse was when I was just a little kid learning to ride."

"I was probably more scared than you, so I hung on tighter," Josh said sympathetically. "If Susie had been the first one down the mountain, I probably would have gotten knocked off by that branch."

"Where are the horses?" Kim asked with concern.

"There's a level area about fifty yards down there," Josh said. "I left Susie there."

"What about Flame?"

"He seemed okay to me. He was munching on some grass."

"Can you help me up?" Kim asked.

"Sure." Josh stood and reached down and pulled her up. She stretched gingerly. "I may be sore in the morning."

"We've been saddle-sore every morning since the first day we got here."

"That would go away if you rode more often," Kim replied with a small smile.

Above them, the sky grew darker with gray rain clouds. Josh hadn't really noticed, but it was still sprinkling. The sprinkle was turning into a shower. The sky rumbled again with thunder. This time it was louder.

"I think it's really going to rain," Josh said.

"I think you're right." Kim looked up uneasily at the sky. "That's not good. We need to get to the horses."

"It's easy to follow the horse tracks down." Josh pointed to the ground.

"Look at the length of some of these tracks." Kim shook her head. "See how they slid in the loose soil and rocks?"

"I can't believe they didn't slip and fall on us."

"Me either," Kim said. "I've never gone down a mountain like that. It was all I could do to hang on. I lost the reins almost as soon as we left the trail. I was holding on to Flame's mane and gripping him with my legs."

"I lost the reins too. I was holding on to the saddle horn. I've got a big blister because I was holding on so tight." He lifted his left hand so she could see the angry red blister in the center of his palm.

"I've heard of people riding down mountains before," Kim said. "But no sane person ever does it. We're lucky none of us ended up with a broken leg or worse. Look how they slid in the dirt."

She pointed at another deep hoofprint in front of them. The horse's slide had made a gash in the ground over two feet long.

When they reached the clearing, the two horses were standing side by side, heads bent, munching contentedly on fresh mountain grass. Neither horse even seemed to notice the two young people. Kim walked over quickly to check on the horses. She bent down, checking Flame's legs. Then she looked at Susie.

"Amazing!" Kim said as she stood back up. She patted Flame on the side. "I see a few scratches but no big cuts or gashes."

"They didn't get bit by that snake, did they?"

"No sign of it," Kim said. "I think there would be swelling if they had."

Josh looked around. Most of the mountain loomed above them. All he could see were spruce and aspen trees. Thunder rumbled. The horses snorted. Rain began to come down harder.

"What do we do now?" he asked the girl.

"Get under that tree," she said, pointing to a big spruce. They led the horses over to it. "Tie the reins to the branches." Kim tied Flame's reins to a low branch. "Lightning can spook them."

As Josh was tying the horse to the tree, the rain began to pour. He undid his saddle roll and got out his poncho. Kim did the same. They huddled under the tree, watching the rain. It poured and poured with periods of strong hail. They waited, watching in silence. After about twenty minutes it was still raining.

"This isn't good," Kim said.

"I'm not getting that wet. It's safe under the tree."

"I don't mean that. We'll never be able to get back up on the trail now. We've come down too far, and it's too steep. With this much rain and hail it will be too muddy and slippery. Even if they wanted to come look for us, they couldn't do it. At least not on their horses."

"Is there another way back?" Josh asked. "Maybe we should just wait here until someone comes."

"Maybe." Kim's forehead wrinkled. They waited under the

tree some more. Finally, the rain began to let up. The horses stamped their feet impatiently.

Josh walked out from beneath the dripping branches of the big spruce tree. He turned and looked up the mountain. Josh cupped his hands around his mouth. "Billy! Carlos! We're down here!" There was no reply.

"I wonder what happened to them," Kim said with a frown. "They might not hear you. We came a long, long way down."

"They probably went for help."

"If they could get around that snake," Kim replied. "Those other horses had to be spooked."

"You're right," Josh said. "I didn't see them go off the trail, did you?"

"I didn't have time to notice much. I was too busy just hanging on. I did see you. But the trail was wider back there behind us. Most horses will stay where they can keep their feet."

"They probably went to get help," Josh said.

"But they don't know the way. The trail up to the lodge splits in several places the higher you go. Colt and the other wranglers know the way."

"Where do the splits lead?"

"Most just come to a dead end. They're used for shorter day rides. But there's really only one way to reach the camp at Eagle Peak."

"So they could be riding and not find the other riders?"

"That's a real possibility," Kim said seriously. "If they had good trail sense, they could follow the tracks of the other riders."

"I don't know if I would assume that," Josh said with soft hesitation. "I mean, none of us are experienced riders. We don't have much trail sense."

"They would have to get past that rattlesnake first. He was right in the middle of the trail. The horses wouldn't go around that snake."

"Maybe they could throw a rock at the snake and get it to move. That's what I would do."

"That would work," Kim agreed. "Would they think of that?"

"I don't know." Josh sighed as he looked up the big mountain.

"Well, for sure we can't go back up the way we came down." Kim looked up the mountain. "Riding off the trails is dangerous. We don't allow it at the ranch. Even our experienced wranglers seldom ride off the trails. But there is one possibility. There may be other trails below us."

"Really?" Josh asked hopefully. "Have you ridden down there before?"

"No." Kim shook her head. "This part of the mountain is all private property. It belongs to the Pierson Mining and Mineral Company. They let the ranch use the upper trail even though it crosses part of their land. But that's it. They don't allow anyone to ride on their land. There are old mines, but they're all closed up. No one is allowed up here except old Ben Tucker."

"Who's he?"

"He's a prospector. He comes out to the ranch every so often when he goes to town. My grandfather knows him. My grandfather says he lives all by himself out here near Corrigan's Ridge."

"You mean the Corrigan who buried his treasure?"

"The same one," Kim said with a half smile. "But I don't believe that legend. Neither does my grandfather."

"You never went looking for the treasure?"

"No way. It's a waste of time. Besides, Pierson Mining and Mineral owns all this land now, including the land where Corrigan had his claim. Like I say, they don't allow people back here to look for lost gold."

"Then what's that sound?" Josh cocked his head. He motioned for Kim to be quiet. Down the side of the mountain they heard a familiar noise.

"That sounds like a truck or car!" Kim said excitedly. "There must be some kind of road down there."

"Does Ben Tucker drive a car?"

"I don't think so. He just has an old mule. But maybe someone else does live down there. And they might have a phone. We could call the camp and tell them where we are. Or we could even call Colt. He carries a cellular phone with him."

"Will it work in the mountains?" Josh asked.

"It depends where you are. But it's worth a try. If we can talk to him, he can tell us what we need to do. And if not, we can at least call my grandfather back at camp."

"Let's go then." Josh looked up the mountain once more. "I wonder what happened to Billy and Carlos."

"I don't know. But let's see if someone lives further down the mountain. If we can make a call, that's our best chance of letting the others know we're all right."

They heard the sound of a car engine again. The sound was more distant, yet still close enough to give the stranded riders hope.

"Let's catch that car!" Josh said eagerly. The two young people ran for their horses.

Chapter Seven

Ghost Town

Kim untied her horse and led him back out into the clearing. Josh followed her. The clearing sloped gently downhill for about forty yards and then dropped off. Kim searched the edge of the clearing for the best way down.

"This will work." She led her horse down past a fir tree. The ground was steep and slick, but Flame followed Kim. Josh looked down. The mountainside was steep. "It's a little muddy, so we'll have to be extra careful going down. There must be a road down here somewhere. There will be a way out."

"Okay," Josh said with less enthusiasm than he felt. "Come on, Susie."

He started down the slippery hillside again, leading the horse. Susie obediently followed. Josh watched his steps carefully. He tried to step on the larger rocks whenever he could to avoid the slippery mud. Overhead, the gray sky threatened to rain again.

Kim pushed past a group of aspens and came out into a clearing. She stopped, waiting for Josh to catch up.

"This must be it!" Kim said with excitement. Josh was disappointed. The road was nothing more than two dirt tracks with grass in the middle. The narrow road, cut into the side of the mountain, looked seldom used, but the tire tracks were fresh. The dirt road was marked by ditches, and small gullies cut across it.

"Water coming down the side of the mountain makes all these cuts in the road." Kim looked at a trickle crossing the road.

"Not much of a road."

"But at least we can ride." Kim leaned down to clean the mud off her boots. "Clean your boots so you don't slip in the stirrups."

Josh tied Susie's reins to a tree branch and sat down. He found a dead branch and used the stick to pry the caked mud off the bottom of the boot. Kim finished before he did. She climbed up into the saddle. Josh grabbed the reins with his left hand and grabbed the saddle horn. He hoisted himself up.

"You're getting better at that," Kim observed.

"Thanks."

"The sound of the car came from the west. Let's go that direction." Kim led the way. She headed down the left track of the dirt road. Josh rode up beside her on the right track. They horses walked quickly down the road.

"Do you think we should go faster?" Josh asked impatiently.

"Not with all these branches hanging down." Kim ducked her head to one side. "Besides, there are too many gullies in this road. I don't want Flame or Susie to step in a hole. They could break a leg."

"You're probably right," Josh said. They rode without speaking. The old road curved in and out, following the side of the mountain. The gray skies kept threatening rain. Kim and Josh rode in silence for a long way. Each time they rounded a bend in the old road, Josh expected to see a car, a cabin or something with people.

"This sure is beautiful country up here," Josh said as he got glimpses of the mountains. In the distance he could see some snow-capped peaks. "Have you lived here a long time?"

"For over five years."

"Where did you live before?" Josh asked.

"In Denver. Then my parents split up."

"Oh," Josh said softly. "Does your mom or dad live near here?"

"No." There was an edge in her voice. "My father is a rodeo rider, and he goes all over the place, mostly in the southwest."

"Do you get to see him very often?"

"Not hardly." Her voice was suddenly bitter.

"Does your mom live at the ranch?"

"No, I live with my grandfather." Kim stared straight ahead. "You live with both your parents, don't you?"

"Yes."

"You're lucky." Kim's voice was hard. Josh waited, wondering if she would say more, but she didn't.

They rode along for more than a half-hour. The road seemed to get more narrow and remote. The tall trees kept them shaded most of the way.

They rounded a curve and the road forked. Kim stopped. The road with the car tracks veered off to their right and went downhill.

"I think we should follow the tracks, don't you?" Kim asked.

"Yes. I just wish we'd get to wherever we're going. People are really going to worry about us."

"We're doing the best we can," Kim said with determination.

They followed the lower road. It curved continuously, sloping gently down the mountainside until the trees weren't so thick.

"We're almost in the canyon now," Kim said as they rode out into an open space. She looked up and pointed. "That far ridge is where the trail riders will camp tonight at Eagle Peak."

"It looks pretty far away," Josh said. They rode around a bend in the road. Josh's mouth dropped open. He stopped his horse. Down below them in the tiny valley were several small shacks and buildings.

"It's like a town," Josh whispered in surprise.

"It *is* a town," Kim whispered back. "But it's a ghost town. No one lives up here."

Josh nodded. As he looked closer, he noticed that the buildings were all made of ancient gray boards. Windows were broken out. Some of the buildings looked so old it seemed like a strong wind could knock them over.

"I hope there are no real ghosts down there," Josh said. As soon as he said it, an olive-green Jeep drove down the main street in the old town.

"That's my grandfather's Jeep with Dr. and Mrs. Matthews! What are they doing here?"

"Let's wait and see. We saw them acting real suspicious back at camp."

"Really? I thought they were acting kind of odd too. I told my grandfather about it, but he said don't worry about it. But I thought he was keeping something from me. He was talking with them the last few days, but he acted like he didn't want me around."

"Really?"

"Yeah," Kim said. "I think he was upset. But he wouldn't say anything about it. He usually tells me what he thinks. But this time, I could tell he didn't want to talk about them. And when he let them use his Jeep, I was really surprised. He never lets anyone use that Jeep. He loves it as much as I love Flame."

"Then why would he let that old couple use it?"

"I don't know," Kim said. "I overheard them talking before they realized I was there, and they mentioned a lot of money."

"They did?"

"I came out of my room, and they didn't know I was in the hall. But I heard them say something about a half-million dollars."

"A half-million dollars!" Josh said.

"That's right. But as soon as I walked in the room, they stopped talking. The old couple acted friendly and said they would talk to my grandfather later. When I asked the man what they wanted, he didn't really answer me. He said he had to go to the stables. He seemed kind of upset."

"They must be looking for Corrigan's gold."

"I didn't think my grandfather believed in the gold."

"You don't think he's mixed up in anything illegal, do you?" Josh asked.

"Of course not. My grandfather is more honest than anyone I know. He always tells the truth."

"But you said he acted suspicious when you asked about the couple. My friend Billy said he saw that couple poking around near the wranglers' bunkhouse. Then we saw them sneak in through the window of that shed where your grandfather keeps his Jeep. We told your grandfather about it. Then they came over. The man whispered something to your grandfather."

"Could you hear what he said?"

"Not a bit," Josh said. "But after that, your grandfather told us not to worry about what we saw. You don't think your grandfather is helping them do something illegal? After all, I thought you said the whole valley is owned by Pierson Mining and Mineral. That couple would be trespassing here in your grandfather's Jeep."

"He wouldn't be involved in anything illegal." Kim frowned.

Even with a frown, her troubled face looked beautiful. Josh gulped, not believing his own thoughts. He was glad no one could overhear him thinking.

"Speaking of suspicious." Kim pointed. The Jeep had stopped. The couple got out and climbed up a small hill. They disappeared behind an old building.

"What do you think they're up to?" Josh asked.

"I don't know. But let's go take a look. If they ask us what we're doing, we can tell them about the snake and getting off the trail."

They led the horses down the road. Once they were in the floor of the valley, the dirt road was smoother. Kim began to trot. Josh nudged Susie with his heels. The big gray horse began to trot. The jerky motion made Josh slap in the saddle. Kim looked over at the slapping sound. She slowed her horse.

Josh pulled back gratefully on the reins.

"You don't know how to trot yet, do you?" Kim said sympathetically.

"I guess not. It's too bouncy."

"You have to bounce with the horse's gait."

"What?"

"Never mind. We can work on it back at the ranch. Let's just keep walking. It will be more quiet."

The little dirt road wound slowly down through the valley. For a moment they lost sight of the old ghost town as they rode behind a stand of cottonwood trees. When they got past the trees, the town came into view. At the same time, a light rain began to fall. The gray sky behind them lit up and then rumbled.

"We're going to get wet again," Josh said glumly.

"I hope there's not much lightning. It makes Flame really nervous."

"Flame sounds like such a courageous name for a horse."

"He's a big chicken when it comes to thunderstorms and rattlesnakes," Kim replied. "Otherwise he's a great horse."

The horses walked through the drizzling rain. Another flat dirt road joined the road they were on.

Kim looked back at the other road, which ran straight east on the valley floor. "I think this road goes all the way to the road that runs by the ranch. They must have come in on this road and been exploring on the other roads."

"They must be looking for the treasure," Josh said. "They had a metal detector with them this morning."

The two riders turned back around. They headed into the town. They slowly rode past the first building on the east end of the ghost town. It was an old wooden shack, leaning heavily to one side. A door on rusted hinges was hanging open. Josh tried to see inside the dark shack. It appeared to be empty.

"This place must be over a hundred years old," Josh whispered.

"At least," Kim replied. They rode down the silent, deserted street. The wet road was totally clear except for the tracks of the Jeep. They passed more shacks and then some taller buildings.

"That must have been a store." Josh pointed to the tallest building, which had a fallen-down porch.

"It could have been a saloon."

"I wish we could look inside. I wonder if we would find anything."

"You couldn't pay me to go into one of those places." Kim looked down the street. "They parked up behind that last building, didn't they?"

"I think so."

Kim nudged her horse so it would walk faster. Josh did the same. He was trying to think what they would say to the old couple as they passed the last building, which appeared to be a barn. They saw tracks but no Jeep.

"Where did they go?" Kim asked.

"I don't know. It looks like they backed up and left. Look, the road goes on and curves out of sight up ahead."

"What were they looking for?"

"Probably that mineshaft." Kim pointed over Josh's shoulder. He turned and saw a dark hole in the side of the hill.

"Let's take a look." Josh pulled his collar up. The sky rumbled again.

"Okay. But let's hurry. It's going to rain hard again." Kim climbed off her horse. Josh did the same. She held the reins, looking for a place to tie up Flame.

"That's a hitching rail, isn't it?" Josh pointed to a wooden post by the side of the barn.

"It sure is." Kim wound the leather straps around the wooden rail. "It looks half rotten, though."

Josh tied Susie to the rail also. The big horse immediately dipped her head, trying to nibble a patch of grass nearby. The leather straps pulled tight, and the old wooden rail creaked.

"Don't eat now, Susie," Josh muttered.

"Let's hurry," Kim said nervously, looking at the sky.

"I can see footprints." Josh pointed at the ground. "They go right to the mine." Josh led the way up the hill, following the footprints in the wet ground. As they stepped under the overhang of the mine, it began to rain harder.

"It's all locked up," Josh said with disappointment. "Look." A huge, rusted metal plate covered the entrance of the mine. A large metal sign was welded to the plate. The edges of the plate were sealed with cement.

"NO TRESPASSING. KEEP OUT! VIOLATORS WILL BE PROSECUTED! Pierson Mineral and Mining Company."

Josh looked carefully around the edge of the rusted plate. He picked up a rock and tapped on the metal. "I don't think anyone has been inside there for years."

"I guess not. That must be why they left. We better get back."

The gray sky rumbled, this time more loudly. Kim jerked her head up. The clouds were dark and looked angry. Suddenly lightning flashed at the far end of the valley. In half a second, loud thunder crashed, echoing through the whole valley.

"Wow!" Josh put his hands over his ears.

"Flame!" Kim started running down the hill. Josh looked up in time to see Kim's chestnut stallion racing out of the far end of town. The big horse galloped as if ghosts were chasing him.

Chapter Eight

Chasing Flame

Kim kept running. Josh ran down the hill after her. Rain began to pour from the sky. Lightning flashed, followed immediately by thunder. The gray sky was filled with rain. Josh slipped as he ran after Kim. He rounded the corner of the old barn. The old hitching rail was broken into two rotted pieces, lying in the dirt. Susie was standing quietly inside the barn, looking out at the pouring rain. Kim had already started to climb into the saddle. He slipped inside the barn, glad to be out of the rain.

"Whoa!" Josh yelled. "You aren't going anywhere without me, are you?"

"I've got to get Flame," Kim said anxiously.

"In the rain? Don't go out there. What if there is more lightning? Besides, it's raining cats and dogs. It will stop soon. Won't Flame just get under a tree somewhere and wait it out?"

"I don't know." For a moment it looked as if Kim would

still ride out into the rain. Then lightning flashed again with a tremendous crack, right outside the door. Susie reared up, her ears flattened back.

"Whoa, whoa, Susie," Kim spoke softly to the horse. Frowning at the downpour, she reluctantly dismounted from the gray mare. "Flame will be terrified of that lightning. Who knows what he'll do?"

"You aren't going to catch up with him in this rain."

"I guess not. But as soon as it stops, we've got to get after him," Kim said with determination.

"I agree." Josh looked up at the sky. The dark clouds were blowing swiftly by. The rain continued to pour. Then it began to bounce on the dirt road. The ground was peppered with what looked like small white marbles.

"It's hailing again!" Kim pointed to the bouncing ice crystals.

"Will it hurt Flame?" Josh asked loudly.

"Not if it stays that small." Kim frowned as she looked up at the angry sky. "Sometimes it can get bigger than baseballs."

The rain and hail pounded down on the rusty tin roof in a dull roar. Water poured through leaking holes all through the barn. Josh moved sideways to avoid one of the little streams. He looked down at the dirty floor of the barn.

"They were in here too." Josh pointed at tracks on the floor. "Or somebody was in here."

"Sure enough. Those are fresh tracks, and they didn't come from you or me. It must have been them. There are two sets of tracks."

"What were they doing up here?" Josh asked. The barn seemed to be totally empty. A few wooden stalls were on the left side. A rusty piece of chain hung from the wall on a rusty nail. Josh walked over to look in the stalls. Whoever had been in the barn had done the same thing. Two sets of footprints walked to and from the stalls.

"No treasure in here." Josh walked back, dodging the leaks that dripped from the roof.

"That roof sure has a lot of leaks." Kim looked up. "At least the rain is beginning to stop."

"I think you're right." The gray clouds were thinning out as blue sky began to peek through. The hail stopped. Then the rain slowed down. Then, almost as suddenly as it had begun, it got quiet.

"Let's go," Kim said. The ground was covered with a thin layer of the small hailstones. She looked up at the sky. The dark clouds were blowing toward the east. "I bet it's raining back at the ranch right now."

Kim looked at Susie and then at Josh. She frowned. Josh could read her thoughts.

"Do you want me to wait here while you go look for Flame?" Josh asked.

"No, we can ride double." Kim put her foot up in the stirrup and mounted the horse. Then she turned and extended her hand.

"I'm not a very good rider," Josh said weakly.

"That's why you'll sit behind me and hold on."

Josh nodded. Kim moved her foot out of the stirrup so he could put his in. She took his arm and pulled as he hopped up. She was strong, he thought as he swung his leg over the broad back of the horse.

"Either hang on to my waist or the saddle," Kim said. Josh picked the saddle. Kim turned Susie and headed west out of the deserted town.

"The rain washed away Flame's tracks," Kim said over her shoulder.

"I don't see any tire tracks either. The hail is kind of pretty."

"Look, the road curves up there." Kim followed it around a long loop on the south side of the ghost town. She watched the dirt, searching for tracks. The road passed behind the weathered buildings. Kim dug her heels into the horse's flank, and Susie began to trot. Josh let go of the saddle and grabbed Kim's waist.

The old road curved and turned back toward the town. It turned down beside the first two shacks at the east end.

"This is just a loop," Josh said. They were on the main street again. Kim slowed Susie down to a walk. "The Jeep must have been going out as we were going in."

"But what about Flame?" Kim looked anxiously around the town. "He probably didn't follow the road at all."

Kim nudged the horse again, and Susie trotted down the main street of the old mining town. They paused in front of the barn.

"He must have kept running toward the west," Kim said. "He was running that way when I last saw him. There are trees up at the far end of the canyon."

Kim followed the road out of town and then left it at the curve. She guided Susie over the flat expanse of the small valley toward the trees at the opposite end of the canyon.

"I don't see anything," Josh said. The rocky ground didn't seem to give any clues.

Kim rode into the grove of trees. She studied the grove, hoping to see her horse standing under one of the tall firs, but all they saw were dripping branches.

They kept riding west. A sheer wall of rock rose before them at the far end of the canyon. Josh looked at the wall, impressed by its size and grandeur.

"This is a beautiful place," Josh said. "It doesn't look like there's any way to go but back the way we came."

"I *have* to find Flame." Kim anxiously studied the landscape. Off to their left she saw a clearing in the trees. She rode south, away from the canyon wall.

"That looks like a trail."

"It sure does." Kim nudged Susie onward. A winding narrow path led up the side of the mountain.

"Would he have come this far?" Josh asked.

"If he was scared enough, he could be in the next county by now. Let's follow this trail a ways. We'll have to walk Susie."

Josh slid quickly off the horse, and Kim followed. She immediately took the reins in her hand.

"Let's hurry." Kim began to walk. Josh admired her determination. The trail, what there was of it, got steeper and more narrow as they climbed higher. Soon it was too narrow for them to walk side by side.

"You want me to lead Susie?" Josh offered.

"No, it's okay. Let's go up higher. Maybe we can get high enough to look down on the valley and spot Flame."

"That might work." Though Josh wondered if that was realistic, he didn't want to discourage Kim. If Flame was standing in some grove of trees, they would never see him.

They climbed higher up the side of the mountain. The trail zigzagged a few times and then came to a clearing. Down below they could see the west end of the old mining town and part of the valley.

"Do you see anything?" Josh searched the valley floor.

"No." Kim sounded disappointed and worried. "Where can he be? I hope he didn't get hurt."

"He came down that mountainside okay. If he could do

that, a little lightning wouldn't hurt him. He's a strong horse."

"I don't know," Kim said. "All they have to do is fall into one hole, and they can break a leg."

Her face looked as dark as the distant gray clouds. Josh wished he could say something to comfort her. He looked up the trail. He didn't see a horse, but he did notice something. A thin gray trickle of smoke rose into the air up above them.

"Smoke!" Josh said. Kim looked.

"That's odd. Who would be lighting fires out here?"

"Would it be from the lightning?" Josh asked.

"It could be. Or maybe it's hikers."

"Let's go check it out. If it's hikers, maybe they've seen Flame. Or maybe we'll get a better look down into the valley from there."

Kim nodded. Once again they headed up the narrow winding trail. For a while Josh lost sight of the smoke. He walked more quickly up the trail. Before he knew it, he was breathing hard from moving so fast in the thin air.

"Slow down," Kim said as they came into another clearing. Josh searched the sky above them. He found the trickle of smoke again. He followed it down.

"A cabin!" Kim said with surprise. Just then a dog began to bark and then howl.

"Let's go," Josh said. The trail led out of the clearing, up through more trees and right to an old log cabin.

"Aren't we still on the mining company's land?" Josh asked.

"I'm pretty sure we are," Kim said slowly.

Up ahead, the door of the cabin opened. An old man stepped out on the porch. He wore blue overalls and a red plaid shirt. A long gray beard hung down to the middle of his chest. He held a long, double-barreled shotgun in his hands.

Chapter Nine

Old Ben Tucker

Ben! Ben Tucker!" Kim yelled out to the old man.

"Set, Buddy, set!" the old man instructed the dog. The big hound lay down obediently at his master's feet, but his eyes were trained on the two strangers below him.

"What in tarnation are you young'uns doing on my side of the mountain?" the old man asked. His voice was a little on the creaky side, but his gray-blue eyes were clear and piercing. He leaned the shotgun against the cabin door.

Kim and Josh walked rapidly up the hillside. Kim tied Susie's reins to the railing of the porch steps. She climbed the steps and gave Ben a short hug. Josh followed her up the steps. He shook the old man's hand.

"You're a long way off the trail," the old man said. "Did the storm blow you off the mountain?"

"Not exactly." Kim began to explain rapidly all that they had been through, from the time they got scared off the trail by the rattlesnake. The old man nodded and listened carefully. He shook his head in amazement.

"Land sakes girl, you two are lucky to be standing here with no broken bones," he cackled. "We better get you back to the trail riders before they have a fit worrying about you."

"But what about Flame?" Kim asked anxiously.

"I figure I can find Flame for you," Ben said. "I have an idea where he might be."

"You can find him, Ben?" Kim asked.

"Child, I've been up in these mountains for fifty years," the old man said. "I've found lost riders, lost hikers, lost skiers, lost horses and lost dogs. Me and Buddy here can find just about anything. He's part bloodhound, you know."

"Let's go then," Kim said. "We've got to find Flame."

"Hold on," the old man said. "That horse ain't going nowhere too far. There's only one way out of that valley, and that's got a fence at the end of it."

"How did that Jeep get in?" Josh asked.

"Well, son," the old man said, "that fence has a gate, and on that gate is a padlock bigger than my fist, and maybe those folks had a key to that lock."

"You mean you think they had permission?" Kim asked.

"Some folks still ask for permission to go on another person's land," the old man said. "They were using your grandfather's Jeep with his permission, weren't they?"

"Yes, but he might not have known what they were up to," Kim said. "Maybe they broke through the fence. If the fence was broken, Flame could get out that end of the valley."

"But you said your horse was running west," Ben replied.

"Well, he was the last time I saw him," Kim admitted.

"Then I have an idea he didn't go back east at all." Ben

turned to Josh. "There's hardly anything as lazy as a horse. They just want to find a nice meadow and eat until their belly is full. No, the first thing we need to do is get you caught up with the trail riders so they don't go all over these mountains looking for you and worrying about you. That's what your grandfather would want."

"I suppose you're right." But Kim didn't look very convinced. "How can we catch up? I don't even know where to go from here."

"I can take you right to them, probably," the old man said. "They usually stop up at Broken Wing Pass around three o'clock, don't they?"

"That's about the time, more or less," Kim said. "They'd be a little slower if the rain held them up."

"Then I'll take you right to them," the old man said.

"But we came way off the trail," Josh said.

"You're on mining company property now, son," the old man replied as he climbed down the porch steps. He pulled out his pocket watch and looked at it. "The trail Horseshoe Ranch rides goes a long way around the mountain. That's pleasure riding. But I know a shortcut. Come on, Buddy. Let's get Myrtle."

"Who's Myrtle?" Josh whispered to Kim.

"Myrtle is my mule," the old man said loudly. Josh grinned. Ben was old, but there was nothing wrong with his hearing.

The old man laughed as he walked around his cabin. The big brown hound followed at his heels. Behind the cabin were a little corral and stable. Ben opened the gate and went into the stable. He walked out leading Myrtle.

Josh stared at the big animal. It looked a lot like a horse, yet its head was shaped differently.

"A mule is part horse and part donkey, isn't it?" Josh asked Kim uncertainly.

"A real mule is a cross between a female horse and a male donkey," Kim replied. "If the father is a horse and the mother is a donkey, they call it a hinny."

Josh stared at the big ears of the mule. The old man quickly put a bridle over her head and a bit in her mouth. Then he put on a saddle.

"Don't you have a phone?" Kim asked suddenly. "I heard you mention that you got one like my grandfather."

"Actually I do," the old man said. "But she's broke. I got one of them modern cell phones, and I talk to my daughter clear in Florida most every weekend. But this last week I knocked it off the table when my hot tea spilt. Broke her good."

"Do you have electricity?" Josh asked, looking back at the cabin, trying to spot power lines.

"Got a generator," the old man said proudly. "That whole cabin is wired for twelve volts. Even my refrigerator. And I got a snowmobile in the stable."

The old man climbed on the mule's back. He turned her head, and she walked down the hill to the trail. He headed her up the trail going west. Kim got in Susie's saddle. She helped Josh up onto the horse's back.

"Did your daddy make it back for Easter?" the old man asked Kim.

"No," she said sullenly. "And he's not coming back this summer at all. He's too busy, he said."

"That's too bad," the old man replied. "I know Dan and you would be mighty glad to see Buck."

"Who's Buck?" Josh whispered.

"Her father!" Ben shouted back. "Son, you don't need to whisper. I'm a plain-spoken man."

"Right," Josh said. The silence was long. They rode upward at a steady pace.

"Did you ever look for Corrigan's gold?" Josh asked.

"Well, of course," the old man said. "Why do you think I stay up in these mountains?" He chuckled.

"I thought the mining company paid you to look after things up here," Kim said.

"Well, that's the other reason I live up here," Ben said and chuckled louder. Josh wondered if the old man was making a joke. Ben's quick wit surprised him. "Mostly I just like it up here. This is God's country, no two ways about it."

"Don't you get lonely?" Josh asked.

"Not with Buddy and Myrtle to keep me company," the old man said. "Besides, I go to town every two weeks or so. And I can talk to my daughter when the cell phone is cranked up right."

"I know where we are now," Kim said. "We're on the trail above Broken Wing Pass. How did we get up here so fast?"

"You just got to know the mountains," the old man said. "Your outfit is still down there cooling their boot heels." Ben Tucker pointed down the hillside. In the small meadow below they could see the horses and riders from the ranch.

"Let's go," Ben said.

He led the way down the trail. The riders were just starting to get on their horses when Ben, Kim and Josh rode into the small clearing.

"There's Billy and Carlos!" Josh said excitedly. "They're talking to Colt."

"Sure enough," Kim said. "They made it."

Billy's mouth dropped down to his chest when he saw Kim and Josh ride Susie into camp. Everyone else was staring at the old man with the long beard riding the mule.

"What happened, Kim?" Colt asked with great concern. "These boys just told me some crazy tale about you going down the side of the mountain. I was about to go look for the broken pieces."

"Wait till you hear what happened," Kim said. She and Josh took turns telling their story to Colt, Pinkey and the other wranglers. They were all surprised.

"We tried to go on foot down the side of the mountain, but decided we should get Colt," Billy said. "Then our horses ran away from us. They ran back down the trail, all the way to the meadow where Billy fell in the river."

"Then we almost took the wrong trail," Carlos added. "We just got here five minutes before you did. I was worried you all had killed yourselves."

"You kids are lucky to be alive, going down the mountain like that." Pinkey whistled. "I never heard of anyone doing that."

"You say that old couple was riding around that ghost town in your grandfather's Jeep?" Colt asked for a second time.

"That's right," Josh said.

"The boy thinks they're looking for Corrigan's gold," Ben said with a twinkle in his eye. He looked at Colt. "What do you think?"

"I thought that road was blocked off by a fence and gate," Colt said. He looked at Pinkey with questioning eyes.

"It sure is, Colt," Pinkey said quickly. "No trespassing signs are posted all over the place. The Pierson Company don't allow no one up there except Ben."

"I guess we'll have to report that to your grandfather too," Colt said with a troubled look. "Some of these city folks can't leave well enough alone. Crazy fools looking for buried treasure. We need to head up the trail or the people at the lodge will think we all fell off the mountain."

"But what about Flame?" Kim asked.

"You two can ride Susie the rest of the way," Colt said. "Then you can take one of the horses up at the lodge. When we get back, Pinkey and I will go look for Flame."

"Ben said he would look for him," Josh offered. "He said he knows where he might be."

"Ben don't need to look for a Horseshoe Ranch horse," Colt said firmly. "That's our problem, and we'll take care of it."

"No problem for Buddy and me." The old man smiled.

"I said we could take care of it, old-timer," Colt replied stiffly.

"My name is Ben Tucker," the old man said without smiling. "And you're the new wrangler from California. I didn't quite catch your name."

"Colt Garrison," he replied, holding out his gloved hand toward Ben. The old man took it and shook. "I don't mean any offense, Mr. Tucker. I just thought Kim's horse is our problem. Right Pinkey?"

"That's right," Pinkey said. "We can get her, Ben. That's the way Kim's granddaddy would want it."

"You don't mind if me and Myrtle ride along with you all up to the lodge?" Ben asked. "Alma and Fred are up there this season, aren't they?"

"That's right, Ben." Pinkey looked at Colt uneasily. "They're old friends of yours?"

"Surely are," Ben replied. "I left my whittling knife up there a few weeks ago, and I've been aiming to go back and get it. Today would be as good a day as any."

"What about my horse?" Kim looked in Ben's face.

"I'm sure these big fellas can round up one pony," Ben said. "And if they can't, I can help them out. But if I was that horse, I know where I'd go. I'd go where all the other horses go to be sociable. Yep, that's what I'd do. Find me a little grass and water in a nice little lost canyon and settle right down. Come on, Myrtle!"

The old man clucked and dug in his heels, and Myrtle the mule started up the trail. Ben looked over his shoulders at the group and smiled, then turned back around.

"What's he talking about?" Josh asked.

"That old coot is half crazy if you ask me." Pinkey spat on the ground. Colt watched the old man for a moment. Then he turned back to Kim.

"Don't worry, Kim," Colt said. "Pinkey and I will make sure you get Flame back. I'm just glad you two are safe. We need to get back on the trail. I'll send Jeff back here to bring up the rear. I don't want any more strays wandering off on this trip."

"I can handle it, Colt," Kim said quickly. "I don't need Jeff."

"I already let you handle it, and look at what happened," Colt said.

"But it was an accident," Kim snapped. "I didn't know a rattlesnake would be in the middle of the trail!"

"I'm not going to argue, Kim," the big man said firmly. His eyes were hard. "I gave you a chance, and look at what happened."

"I can handle it!" Kim insisted, trying to control the tone

of her voice.

"You don't even have a horse," Colt said condescendingly. "You let him run away."

"She can ride Susie," Josh offered. "In fact, I was going to ride with Billy on Samantha the rest of the way or walk."

"I don't have to ride at all," Kim said. "I can walk."

"She can ride Susie, and I'll double with Billy," Josh said helpfully. "That will work. It's not that far to the lodge, is it?"

"Another three hours in the saddle," Colt said. "I don't care how you saddle up. But I want everyone on a horse. This is a trail ride. And I'm still sending Jeff back here to bring up the rear. Do you want to stand out here and argue with me, Kim? I already have a whole lot to tell your grandfather, when we get back, about you falling down the side of the mountain. Do you want me to add to the list?"

Kim stared with cold fury at the ground. The big cowboy frowned. He looked uneasily at Josh and the others. Colt turned and rode off, not waiting for a comment.

Chapter Ten

The Campfire at Eagle Peak

Kim looked up when Colt rode off. She stared after him with her eyes squinted in hard, angry slits.

"Colt!" Kim yelled. But Colt kept riding. Kim mumbled to herself. When she saw Josh staring, she looked away. When she turned back, her eyes were wet with tears.

"I don't care if you ride Susie," Josh said softly. "Really I don't."

"It's not that." Kim tried to keep her voice under control. She wiped the corners of her eyes quickly with her shirt-sleeve. "It's just that Colt can be so . . . so . . ."

"Bossy?" Billy offered.

"Yeah," Kim said. "But it's like he has it in for me too. I don't know. I know he's a expert rider and all, but I wish my grandfather had never hired him. Everyone said he was so great with horses."

"Isn't he?" Josh asked. "I saw him taming that horse the other day at the corral, and that bronc couldn't throw him."

"He's a good rider," Kim admitted. "But I think he breaks a horse too hard. You can break a horse without breaking its spirit. I've seen Colt really get angry at a horse. He takes it too personal, like he's got something to prove to the horse and to the world. We had a really great new horse that he just rode into the ground and broke her spirit, I think."

"What does your grandfather say?" Josh asked.

"He's so busy, he doesn't hang around the stables like he used to," Kim replied. "He hired Colt because of his reputation. I told Colt I thought he was being too hard on the horse. Ever since then, he's had it in for me. The great champion Colt Garrison can't be told by anyone, least of all by some little girl, that he's doing something wrong."

Kim's eyes were wet. Her voice was choked with frustration.

"I'm sorry he doesn't like you," Josh said.

"My father recommended him to my granddad," Kim said. "He and Colt used to ride in the same rodeos. Colt even looks like my dad."

"Is your dad at the ranch?" Billy asked brightly.

"No," Kim said miserably. She wiped her eyes. "Here comes Jeff. We better start riding."

"So who wants me to ride with them?" Josh asked Billy and Carlos. "We could take turns, I guess, and I could ride with either one of you."

"Josh is the biggest, and he should ride in front," Kim said using her instructor voice.

"But if I ride behind him, I won't be able to see very good,"

Billy said. "Can I ride with Carlos?"

"Sure," Kim said. "Just do it quick, because Jeff has the patience of a half-lit firecracker."

"Colt told me to get y'all moving," Jeff announced with his Texas accent.

Josh got on Billy's horse and Billy sat behind Carlos.

"Samantha's a friendly horse, don't worry," Billy reassured Josh.

"Josh is a good rider," Kim said. "You should have seen him go down that mountain. He hung on better than I did."

"I was probably just more scared," Josh said with a half-smile.

"Let's hit the trail." Jeff watched the young people. Kim nodded and set off. Josh pulled in behind. Carlos and Billy followed. Jeff brought up the rear. The trail was wider. Kim stopped Susie and motioned for Josh to come ride beside her.

"Thanks for letting me ride Susie," Kim said. "She's a real good horse. That's why we let people without much riding experience ride her."

"You mean greenhorns like me," Josh quoted.

"I'm sorry I said that," Kim said softly. "I do get irritated if people come up here and mistreat a horse and act like they know all about riding when they don't. Last week a man from Kansas and his bratty kids came here, and they rode off the path and were real rough on the horses and wouldn't obey the rules. One of the man's sons, a fourteen-year-old monster named Dale, deliberately rode one of our gentlest horses off the trail and began to gallop. The horse stepped in a hole and broke his leg. He had to be destroyed."

"The monster kid?"

"No, the horse," Kim said bitterly. "It was a bad break. I

could hardly bear it. Colby was a wonderful horse and only six years old."

"What happened to the kid?"

"He only sprained his arm," Kim said angrily. "Now his father is threatening to sue the ranch."

"Sounds like a real jerk."

"I've called him a lot of other names. But what made it worse was that Colt said I should have been watching this kid and prevented the accident. But I couldn't stop him. The kid just took off. I yelled at to him come back. But he didn't listen. He never followed instructions. He thought he knew it all. Apparently he had a few riding lessons back in Kansas and thought he was John Wayne."

"I'm sorry to hear about the horse," Josh said sympathetically. "Why would Colt blame you?"

"Because he doesn't like me and wants me off the trail and out of the stables," Kim said. "I don't trust him. I know I saddled Susie right the other day, before you fell."

"You think Colt had something to do with it?" Josh asked with surprise.

"Yes, I do. I know that sounds like I'm trying to avoid the blame, but I asked the other wranglers some questions yesterday. No one but me and Colt handled Susie before you got her. And I know I saddled her right. I've saddled her for years. I think Colt loosened the cinch strap on purpose."

"Colt seemed real friendly to me."

"He always acts that way around the ranch guests," Kim spat out. "He's always smiling and helping women up on their horses. But they don't know him. When that kid broke Colby's leg, Colt blew up at me."

"That must have been a hard thing to see."

"It was awful. When Colby broke his leg, he screamed out almost like a person. I'll never forget that sound or the sight of him lying there, struggling to get up."

"I'm sorry." Josh didn't know what to say. They rode in silence for a while.

"I can't believe Colt called us 'strays' like we were some kind of wayward cattle," Kim said suddenly. Her voice was angry. "He's been touchy ever since that time I told him he was too hard on that horse. He holds a grudge, and it's not fair."

"Life is too short for grudges. That's why I'm glad for God's grace and forgiveness."

"That's the third time I've heard that," Kim said, turning to look directly at Josh. Her tone was almost accusing. "Did my grandfather tell you to say that to me?"

"Say what to you?" Josh asked in surprise.

"That stuff about grace and forgiving. I thought grace was something you said before you ate a meal. But last week my grandfather gave me a big lecture on forgiveness. Then the pastor at the church in town mentioned it to me after the Sunday church service. Now you're talking about it."

"No one told me to say anything to you about it. Honest."

"I just don't want to be preached at," Kim said defiantly. "My grandfather was telling me all about grace and forgiveness the day after my dad called."

"Your dad?"

"Last week my dad called and said he wasn't going to come visit this summer, that his schedule was too busy," Kim said sharply. "My grandfather acts like I should be all happy and forgiving. It's not fair. How can you forgive someone when they break a promise?"

Kim looked at Josh, demanding an answer. The young man

was overwhelmed by her sudden rush of bitterness.

"When someone breaks a promise, it's hard to forgive," Josh finally said.

"Especially when they've broken lots of other promises," Kim spat out. "He's told me he's coming other times and then never showed up. He just calls on the phone and tells me a bunch of excuses. I don't even care anymore."

She stared straight ahead, her eyes wet. Josh's heart ached, feeling her turmoil.

"Do you ever see your mother?" Josh asked, trying to change the subject.

"Not hardly," Kim grunted. "She's worse than my dad. She left home when I was five. I've never seen her since. I don't know if she's dead or alive. My grandfather says he thinks she lives back east somewhere in Connecticut or Massachusetts. She never calls or writes. Not even a Christmas card. Someday, when I'm old enough to drive a car, I'm going to go find her and tell her what I think of her."

"You've had a rough time," Josh said.

"Yeah, and my grandfather tells me about God and stuff and how I need to forgive," Kim said. "I'd like to see him forgive when someone treats you like dirt."

Josh didn't know what to say. He rode along in silence, praying inside for his heartbroken companion.

They soon passed the timber line. At that altitude the air was too thin for trees to grow. The landscape was eerily empty, just mountain grass and shrubs, rocks and boulders, and patches of snow in the shady spots.

They reached the lodge at Eagle Peak on the Continental Divide just before dark. The air was very chilly. They could see their breath. The hot food in the lodge tasted extra delicious to Josh. Kim ate by herself in the corner of the lodge. Josh watched her with an ache in his heart. He wanted to sit with her, but she acted as if she wanted to be alone.

Later, people gathered outside around campfires, to talk and toast marshmallows. Josh was surprised when Kim came over and sat down next to him. Carlos sat down very close to the fire. Billy brought out a guitar.

"Hey, Josh." Billy gave Josh the guitar. "I found this inside the lodge. They said we could use it. Why don't you lead us in some songs?"

"Can you really play?" Kim asked eagerly. "I love guitar music."

"I can play okay." Josh tuned the guitar. It wasn't nearly as good as the guitar he had back home, but the notes sounded true.

Josh strummed some chords and started singing "Home on the Range." Old Ben Tucker came over and joined in the song with his creaky voice. Then to his surprise, Ben pulled out a harmonica and played along with Josh. The harmonica sounded wonderful with the guitar. Josh played more favorites, like "Oh Susannah" and other campfire songs. Ben kept right up with him.

"Sing one of your songs," Billy said. "Josh writes good songs."

"Naw, I don't want to," Josh said shyly. He glanced up at Kim. She was looking right at him. Her eyes shone brilliantly, reflecting the flames of the campfire.

"I'd like to hear one of your songs," Kim said sincerely.

"Really?" Josh replied.

"Why are you so shy here?" Billy demanded. "Back home you're not this shy."

"Would you please," Josh asked, turning to Billy, "just

let me think a moment?"

"No need to get touchy," Billy said. "I like other songs too."

"Sing that song you wrote about the angels singing," Carlos said.

Josh nodded. He felt nervous because Kim was watching, but he began singing anyway. By the end of the song, he didn't feel nervous anymore. Everyone was quiet for a moment.

"You wrote that, young fella?" Old Ben asked. Josh nodded. "You've got some talent there. Got any more?"

Josh sang three more songs. On the last song, once Ben figured out the melody, he played a counterpoint that fit the song beautifully.

"I want to sing some songs we all know," Josh said.

"You know any hymns, like 'My God and I'?" the old man asked.

"I know 'Amazing Grace'." Josh began to strum the guitar softly. Ben played along with him, his eyes shut as he blew out the reedy notes. As the children began to sing, other riders came out of the darkness and stepped closer to the fire to join in. Josh was surprised. They had drawn quite a crowd. It seemed like half the camp was there by the last verse. The comfort of the song drew people in like a warm quilt on a cold mountain night.

"I once was lost but now am found, was blind but now I see," their voices rang out in the clear mountain air. Old Ben played the chorus on the harmonica once more as Josh strummed the guitar. The sound couldn't have been better.

Everyone was quiet as the song ended. People drifted away as quietly as they had come. Ben stood up and stretched.

"That's the finest singing I've joined in in a long time," the old man said. "I think me and Buddy will go bed down now.

Night all." The old man hummed "Amazing Grace" as he walked into the darkness.

Soon only Billy, Carlos, Josh and Kim were left around the dwindling campfire. Josh looked up.

"We'll see you back at the bunkhouse," Carlos said to Josh.

"You coming?" Billy asked.

"Come on." Carlos tugged Billy's arm.

"I was just asking if Josh was coming with us—what's so bad about that?" Billy demanded. Carlos pulled Billy by the arm. The two boys walked off toward the bunkhouse, chattering away. Josh felt totally peaceful. Singing his own songs in front of Kim had finally broken his nervousness.

"You sing and play really well," Kim said. "I wish I played an instrument. Maybe I could get Ben to teach me the harmonica."

"He's really good on that thing," Josh said. For the first time on the whole trip he didn't feel nervous around Kim. Finally, she didn't seem so strange or unusual. She pulled the blanket up around her shoulders.

"I've sung 'Amazing Grace' before, but somehow it seemed different tonight," Kim said.

"That's what makes it a classic song," Josh said. "Most every time I sing that song, I see something new about God's love or realize something about myself that I never saw before. It just kind of happens. It's odd."

"It's a good song," Kim agreed. "It makes me feel really peaceful."

She looked up at the stars in the broad night sky. Josh looked with her. The air was clear and crisp. Whenever he exhaled, little clouds of vapor came out of his mouth.

"I don't think I've ever seen so many stars," Josh said

finally. "Or so far out into the heavens. It looks like you can actually see right into eternity."

"That's the way it is up here above the timberline," Kim said. "Every time I'm up here and look up it seems different. Just like that song. You can't get tired of it."

Josh looked over at her. The firelight cast a warm golden glow on her face and blond hair. She was the most beautiful girl Josh had seen in his whole life. She turned and looked at Josh. The logs on the fire crackled as they burned.

"Thanks for listening to me today," Kim said. "I know it's not your problem, but it helps to have someone to talk to."

"Sure," Josh said. Kim smiled at him. She reached over and took his hand and squeezed it gently. Josh nodded and squeezed her hand back. For a long moment neither of them said a word. Josh felt as if he never wanted to let go of her hand. In the distance, a door slammed. He smiled and released her hand.

"We better get back," Josh said. "Morning will come early."

"It sure will." Kim seemed as self-conscious as her friend.

Josh poured a few buckets of water on the fire and stirred it well. The coals hissed as steam rose up into the cool mountain air. As they walked slowly back toward the lodge, they passed the corral.

"What's that noise?" Josh whispered.

"Sounds like the horses are spooked," Kim whispered back. "Most everyone has gone to bed. We better check it out."

She ducked through the wooden rail fence and walked among the horses. Josh was right behind her. There was only half a moon to light their way.

"I tell you, we got to keep that old man out of there," a

voice whispered. Kim held her finger up to her lips.

"That old coot don't know anything," another voice replied. It sounded like Colt Garrison.

"But he knows about the canyon and the horses."

"You have permission from the mining company to graze the horses," Colt replied.

"But what if the girl's horse is in with the other horses like he said?" Pinkey grunted. "You know that's what he meant."

"Then it makes her horse that much easier to find," Colt said. "We bring back the horse, no problem."

"I still don't like it," Pinkey replied. "I don't want him snooping around down in that Lost Canyon. He might see too much. I say we go down there tonight and bring Kim's horse back. Then old Ben won't need to go down there and snoop around and get suspicious."

"If you go down there and bring back her horse in the middle of the night, then he will get suspicious," Colt said. "It's best to stick to our plan."

"I still think I should go down there and make sure that black shoe polish ain't worn off," Pinkey said. "In fact, the rain might have washed it off, don't you think? I say we use the mine, like we planned, and avoid trouble. We can tell Mr. Paloma to pay and get out of here. I don't want our deal to go sour."

"If it makes you feel better, go down there and put him in the mine," Colt said. "The moon is full. And make sure you don't use your light till you get out of sight of the lodge. Take the rifle just in case."

"You think that old couple was up to anything?" Pinkey asked as he climbed up on the horse. He held a large flashlight in one hand, but the light was not turned on.

"They're just looking for lost gold like all the other old

fools," Colt said. "You worry too much. In a couple of days we'll both be rich men. Now keep quiet as you ride, especially when you ride back in."

Kim pulled Josh back into the shadows as the horses began to rustle again. In the moonlight, Pinkey led his horse out of the corral. Josh's eyes were fixed on the long rifle sticking out of the saddle. Pinkey rode down the trail. Colt closed the corral gate and walked back up to the small bunkhouse where the wranglers spent the night. He closed the door.

"Come on," Kim whispered. She took Josh by the hand and led him toward the trail. "This way!"

They crept behind some rocks and peeked around them. Down below they suddenly saw the big flashlight turn on. They watched in silence as the light bounced along until Pinkey rode around some trees and out of sight.

Chapter Eleven

Lost Canyon

After breakfast, the four children found old Ben packing up Myrtle out by the corral.

"Ben, we know something is going on," Kim said. "Pinkey rode out of here last night after everyone went to bed." Kim quickly told him the story. The old man listened eagerly as he saddled up his mule. "Pinkey is back this morning," Kim said. "But I wonder what he did. They're up to no good, and Mr. Paloma back at the ranch is in on it."

"I wonder what they would want with black shoe polish," the old man mused, pulling on his beard.

"Do you think they found Corrigan's treasure and are trying to hide it?" Josh asked. "Like cover it with shoe polish?"

"Don't know," the old man said.

"I didn't see any horses in the canyon," Kim said.

"That's because you were in the wrong canyon," the old

man replied. "At the west end of Corrigan's Canyon there is a narrow path that leads into Lost Canyon."

"Lost Canyon? Where?" Josh asked. "We rode to the very end of Corrigan's Canyon. It ended with a big rock bluff. I didn't see any passageway."

"That's why they call it 'lost,' " the old man said with a twinkle in his eye. "You got to look a bit to know how to get back in there."

"You think Flame found his way into this other canyon?" Kim asked.

"Probably," the old man said. "A horse can smell other horses. I'm figuring that smart horse of yours found his way into the Lost Canyon and is grazing on green grass right now with those horses."

"But why do they think you would be suspicious if you went to find Flame?" Josh asked. "They said they had permission to graze horses in there."

"They do have permission," the old man replied. "The Pierson Company told me about it. Lots of ranchers around here have used that old canyon over the years to graze horses. It's a nice safe place. Good grass. Got a spring-fed pool for water."

"Then what's going on that they're so worried about?" Kim asked.

"I think that's what I need to figure out," the old man replied with a twinkle in his eye. "I'll go the short way down there and take a look see."

"Can we come?" Kim asked.

"You better stay with the trail ride," the old man replied. "I know a shortcut to the canyon. There's a trail over to the north that takes you right down to it the back way."

"What about my horse?" Kim called out.

"If I find him, I'll bring him back," the old man called back. "I'll see you at the ranch."

Old Ben Tucker rode off on his mule Myrtle. When he got to the trail, he headed north instead of going east. Josh watched the man and mule amble along the barren landscape above the timberline until they disappeared behind some tall boulders.

Back at the corral, Josh found Susie. He took the horse from Colt. The tall cowboy seemed preoccupied. Josh waited around, fiddling with the saddle. He and Susie stood behind two other horses, away from Colt. When Pinkey rode over, the smaller, skinny cowboy seemed agitated.

"I think that old man is up to something. He left not too long ago," Pinkey said to Colt.

"Where did that old man get to?" Colt asked.

"I don't know," Pinkey said. "But what if he starts looking around down in that canyon?"

"You used the mine, didn't you?" Colt asked.

"I sure did," Pinkey said. "But what if he's there?"

"The old coot!" Colt spat out. "Here's what we do. We head down the trail. At Broken Wing Pass, you go on down to the canyon. Get Flame and bring him back. Show the old man the horse if he's around. That should satisfy him, and he'll go back to his cabin."

"But what if he—"

"Then take the rifle with you," Colt interrupted. "You hang around until he leaves. If he starts snooping around too much, then take care of him. There's lots of places in that old mine where an old man like him could disappear, permanently."

"Are you sure, Colt?" Pinkey's voice was frightened.

"He don't have a gun with him," Colt said in disgust. "I think you can handle that old geezer."

"Sure I can," Pinkey said.

Josh walked Susie out of the corral, hoping that Colt wouldn't see him. Pinkey rode past without noticing him. The short cowhand rode down to the front of the line of riders getting ready to go down the mountain.

Outside the corral, Josh waved at Kim. Smiling, she rode over on a pinto pony.

"They're letting me ride Wanda Jean." Kim nodded at the pinto. "She's a little temperamental, but I can handle that."

"We've got to do something," Josh said. "I just heard Colt and Pinkey making a plan to ambush Ben Tucker if he gives them trouble."

Kim began to look scared when Josh told her what he had overheard. Josh waved Billy and Carlos over. His two friends listened attentively as he retold what he had heard.

"We've got to warn Ben," Kim said.

"But how can we do it without being noticed?" Josh asked. "Pinkey will be going down the same trail."

"Not if we leave from here," Kim said. "We can go north, like Ben did, and catch up and warn him."

"You don't think they'll see us?" Josh asked.

"We can ride up over the ridge and around behind the lodge," Kim said. "If Billy and Carlos get in the middle of all the riders, Colt will probably think we're with them."

"It might work," Josh said.

"But I want to go with you guys!" Billy saw he was going to be left out.

"We need you to be with the group," Josh said. "If we're all gone, they'll miss us right away. Please do it."

"Josh is right," Carlos said. "You two need to go warn Ben."

"Let's go," Kim said. "Colt and Pinkey are still busy at the corral with all the other wranglers and riders. The sooner we get behind the lodge the better."

"See you back at the ranch," Josh said to his two friends.

"I hope so," Billy said, still clearly disappointed.

"Follow me." Kim turned her horse and rode toward the hill. She rode behind the lodge and then looked down at the corral. Neither Pinkey nor Colt seemed to have noticed their leaving.

"Let's go." Kim went down the dip in the mountain at a trot. Josh followed. They reached the row of big boulders and saw the hoofprints of Myrtle in the rocky soil. Kim looked back. They could see the roof of the lodge but no other riders.

"We made it." She smiled. "Let's go."

They headed down the trail. Kim rode as fast as she could without putting her horse in danger. The mule tracks were easy to follow. They rode for over ten minutes before they saw him. Buddy barked. The old man stopped and turned to look. He waved at the children. They rode up quickly.

"What in tarnation are you two doing?" Ben asked with surprise.

"We overheard them talking again," Kim said breathlessly. She quickly told Ben about Colt and Pinkey's intentions.

"He had a gun in his saddlebag," Josh added.

"He's going to go down from Broken Wing Pass?" Ben asked.

"That's what he said," Josh replied.

The old man smiled. "Well, we can be in and gone before he ever gets there. Come on, Myrtle." The old man urged the mule onward.

"Are you sure?" Kim asked.

"This is the short way down to Lost Canyon," Ben said. "If he comes from Broken Wing Pass, it will take him an hour longer at least."

The children rode down the steep trail in silence. The old trail was rocky and obviously seldom used. By riding steadily, they reached the level ground of the valley a lot more quickly than Josh had thought possible.

"Only two ways into Lost Canyon, and neither one is easy to find." Ben led them through a small passageway between two sheer rock cliffs at the west end of the canyon.

"No wonder no one can find this place." Josh looked at the narrow strip of sky above them. The riders had gone over thirty yards in the winding, narrow passageway before they rounded a bend. On the other side, they entered Lost Canyon.

"Wow! This place is beautiful," Josh said. Steep mountains surrounded the tiny canyon, which was just half a mile long.

"There's the horses!" Kim pointed straight ahead. A large wooden rail fence made a long, lazy half-circle through the middle of the tiny valley. The rear wall of the big corral was the steep north wall of the canyon. Inside the corral were a few dozen grazing horses. A hawk flew high overhead. The canyon was still and peaceful. The grass still glistened with morning dew.

As they rode to the nearest end of the split-rail fence, Kim cried out suddenly. "There's Flame!" Her horse was at the far east end of the canyon. He still wore his saddle. He was joining two other horses in a morning snack near a pool of water.

"Pinkey was down here, all right," Ben said as they rode forward.

"How can you tell?" Josh asked.

"How else did that horse get inside the fence?" the old man asked.

They rode around the fence until they came to a gate. Ben climbed off his mule and opened the gate. Once they were inside, he closed it.

Kim galloped over to Flame. The big horse raised his head. Kim jumped off her horse and ran to the big chestnut stallion. She wrapped her arms around his neck. She reached into her shirt pocket and gave him a lump of sugar.

"You bad thing!" she scolded softly. "Don't you ever run away again."

"He's bleeding." Josh pointed at his left front leg.

"Oh, no!" Kim said. A nasty gash several inches long glistened with sticky blood. She took the reins and tugged. The horse followed her, but it was obvious that the leg with the cut was causing him pain.

"He is hurt." Kim bent over to look more closely. "But it's not broken."

"You shouldn't ride him on a leg like that." Ben studied the cut. "But he'll heal soon enough, I reckon."

Josh looked at the other horses. Some of them had raised their heads to inspect the strange visitors.

"I don't see anything too unusual, do you?" Josh asked.

"Not out here," the old man said. "Maybe we should go look at the mine."

"What mine?" Kim asked.

"The one over by the north wall," the old man replied. "Leave the animals here."

Kim and Josh followed the old man across the canyon floor toward the sheer cliffs of the north wall.

"The mining company covered up all the old mineshafts." The old man walked along the base of the north wall. He pointed to gray, weathered boards partially hidden by some scrub pines. As they walked closer around a big boulder, they could see the mine entrance. A heavy wood-plank door covered the front of the shaft. No sign or plaque was on this mineshaft saying to keep out.

"This is the only mine in the canyon." Ben looked down at the ground.

"I see two sets of tracks," Josh said. "One is made by boots."

"And the other is a horse," Kim said in surprise. The tracks led right up to the weathered door of the mineshaft.

"Let's take a look inside." Ben pulled on the edge of the old wooden door, but it wouldn't budge.

"It's stuck." Josh tried to help the old man, but the door still wouldn't move.

Ben stepped back and looked carefully at the edge of the door. He ran his finger along the edges.

"Here's the keyhole. Now where's the key, I wonder?" The old man looked on the ground. He looked to the right of the mine door and then the left. Then he smiled. Lying off underneath a bush he saw a rusty crowbar.

He placed the crowbar between the edge of the door and the hard rock. He pushed forward. The rusty old hinges squeaked in protest, but the heavy wooden door slowly creaked open.

"A horse!" Kim said. Standing right on the other side was a large stallion, black as midnight.

"Here boy," Kim said softly. A loose rope halter was fastened around the stallion's head. Kim led him out into the sunlight. The stallion seemed eager to follow.

"That is a really big horse." Josh whistled.

"He *is* a big one," old Ben said.

"But why would they keep him in the mine?" Josh asked.

"Because this is a valuable horse," Kim said. "Look at him. He must be stolen. This is a thoroughbred. I've never seen a horse this fine. I mean, this is a really good horse."

"He is really big." Josh suddenly felt like he knew nothing about horses again.

Kim led the magnificent horse farther out into the open. She stared at him. A strange expression crossed her face. Suddenly she untied her neckerchief and wadded it up. She walked quickly over to the horse and rubbed his broad, flat forehead. A patch of white began to appear.

"What is that black stuff?" Josh asked.

"Shoe polish," Kim said. "They're covering up this marking on his head."

"Why?"

Kim rubbed harder. The white patch slowly took the shape of a crooked, but recognizable, white star. Kim stared at the white star as if she couldn't believe it.

"What is it?" Josh asked.

"Don't you recognize this horse?" Kim asked in a whisper. She kept staring at the horse as if he were a ghost.

"No," Josh said. "Why should I?"

"This horse is one of the most famous horses in the world," Kim replied. "This is Dancing Grace. I'm sure of it. I've seen pictures of him in magazines. Didn't you read about him in the newspapers or see him on television?"

"No," Josh said.

"This horse is supposed to run in the Kentucky Derby later

this year," Kim said excitedly. "He is favored to win. Most people say he could become a Triple Crown winner. They say he's the best horse since Seattle Slew."

"Whoa," Josh said softly. "Then what's he doing here? He's a long way from Kentucky."

"He's not from Kentucky," Kim said excitedly. "He's from California. He's owned by a rich woman named Grace Adams. She owns a whole stable of thoroughbreds, but he's her best horse."

"He's still a long way from home," Josh said.

"Don't you read the news?" Kim asked. "This horse was stolen three weeks ago. He disappeared without a trace. I saw him on the television news and in the newspaper. The police said they had no clues."

"I heard about this horse on my radio." Ben patted the black, muscular flank. "This is one piece of prime horseflesh, anyone can see that. You say he's a race horse?"

"He's beautiful." Josh looked at the horse with new admiration.

"That must be why Colt came here," Kim said. "He didn't care about working at this ranch. He must have been planning this with Pinkey for a long time. He was just hanging around, hiding out and hiding this horse."

"Mr. Paloma must be buying him for a half-million dollars," Josh said. "That's a lot of money for one animal."

"He'd be worth a lot more than that if he won the Triple Crown." Kim patted the big horse's neck. She reached into her shirt pocket and offered a white sugar lump to the big horse. He nibbled eagerly and nuzzled her hand, looking for more. Kim smiled with delight.

"We better get out of here," Josh said nervously. "You can

feed him sugar lumps later. Pinkey's coming, remember?"

"The boy's right," Ben said. "We better get a move on."

"We have to take Dancing Grace with us!" Kim said. "We can't leave him here. What if they get here before we can bring help? We have to take him with us."

They led the big stallion over to the fence where the other horses were tied up. Kim started to take the reins off Wanda Jean.

"What are you doing?" Josh asked.

"I'm going to saddle up Dancing Grace," she said. "This old rope halter is no good. It might break."

"Do you think that's the best way?" Josh asked Ben.

"That old halter could break." Ben nodded. He stared at the big black stallion with curious appreciation. "Hard to believe one horse is worth so much money."

"Maybe you should just saddle Dancing Grace and ride him out," Josh said.

"I guess I could," Kim said nervously. "Do you think I dare? I've only dreamed of riding horses like him."

"Well, sometimes your dreams come true," Josh said. "He's still just a horse, isn't he? In fact, he might rather be ridden than be pulled along. What if he got away while you were leading him?"

"Do you think I should?" Kim asked Ben anxiously.

The old man smiled. "I think you better make up your mind real soon. We need to keep moving. I want to be long gone when those other fellas discover that someone took their million-dollar horse."

Kim hurriedly took the saddle and tack off Wanda Jean. She placed the saddle blanket carefully over the back of Dancing Grace. The big, noble horse waited patiently while she put the saddle on his back. He stamped his foot.

"Hold his reins for me," Kim told Josh. "And feed him some of these while I adjust the saddle."

Kim handed Josh a handful of sugar cubes. Josh offered the big horse one of the sweet white cubes. The warm soft lips nibbled up the sugar greedily.

"He likes it." Josh felt uncomfortable holding the reins of a million-dollar horse. He fed him another cube. The other horses near Josh saw the sugar cubes and walked rapidly toward him.

"It's like a horse convention around here." Josh looked at the approaching horses. He offered a cube to the nearest horse, a brown and white pinto.

Dancing Grace snorted his disapproval and sudden jealousy.

"Hold him still," Kim said firmly. "Western saddles are heavier than racing saddles. He probably isn't used to them. I'm almost done." She quickly tightened the cinch. She checked everything. Then she looked up, surprised to see all the other horses gathered around them.

"Shoo! Shoo!" Josh said helplessly as the hungry horses crowded in closer. "No more sugar. Ben, what do I do?"

"Try not to let them step on you," the old man chuckled, backing up.

"Keep holding Dancing Grace," Kim instructed. Josh nodded. He wrapped the reins around his hand. Kim put her foot in the stirrup. She hopped and pulled herself up into the saddle. The big horse stamped and took a few steps backward, pulling his head. The other horses shied back.

"Good boy, nice fella!" Josh cooed up at the big horse. Dancing Grace stared at Josh. The big horse seemed to like the soothing words and stopped jerking his head. The other horses pressed back in.

"He must like you." Kim smiled. "Look how fast he quieted down."

"They all like me," Josh said as the other horses, wanting some sugar, began to crowd back around him. The pinto nuzzled Josh in the back. Kim's chestnut stallion was right beside him, hoping to get the next cube.

"Flame is probably jealous," Kim said with a grin as she sat straight in the saddle.

"I think he—"

Blam! A rifle shot suddenly split the air, the sound echoing throughout the canyon. Birds flew from the trees. Josh looked up. Pinkey had just ridden into the canyon. The surprised cowhand stopped his horse and aimed the gun toward them.

"Don't nobody move and no one will get hurt!" Pinkey shouted. Aiming the gun at them, the skinny cowboy began riding closer.

Chapter Twelve

Dancing Grace

I'll be dogged," Ben said softly. "That rascal came the short way down here. How did he know? He must have followed our trail. Get on the horse, son."

"What?" Josh asked. "I can't see anything. There's too many horses."

"Get on, right now," Ben said softly. "Pull him up, Kim."

The girl did as she was told. Josh hurriedly pulled himself up. He was thoroughly surprised when Kim moved back so he could sit in the saddle in front of her.

"Hold the reins tight and don't let go," Kim whispered over his shoulder as she gave him the reins.

Josh gripped the reins reluctantly. Up on the big horse's back he could finally see. A shiver of fear coursed down his back. At the west end of the canyon, Pinkey rode slowly toward them, holding his rifle at his shoulder. Josh couldn't tell who exactly he was aiming at, but he didn't want to find out.

"Don't make me shoot again!" Pinkey yelled as he rode closer. He was almost to the gate.

The other horses, crowded around Josh and Kim, and held their heads high, sniffing the air, as they watched the approaching rider. The gunshot had gotten their attention too. A few horses snorted and stamped their feet uneasily. They began to move about nervously as Pinkey rode closer. Ben's dog, Buddy, began to growl, the hair on his back standing up.

Josh felt frozen as he held on tightly to the reins. The big horse stamped his feet. All the horses could sense fear in the air.

"What do we do?" Kim whispered nervously.

"I don't know," Josh said. "He's got a gun."

"Hold on to those reins, boy," the old man whispered. "When I say so, take off and ride toward the east end of the canyon. Don't stop and don't look back."

"But he has a gun!" Kim whispered.

"He's not going to shoot a million-dollar horse," the old man said.

"Don't y'all move!" Pinkey yelled out as he rode closer. He was only thirty yards away. His voice cracked. The young cowhand looked confused and a little scared. "You stay right where you are, old-timer, and no one will get hurt."

Buddy growled. Dancing Grace jerked his head. He could sense the fear of the other horses. He stamped his feet and began walking.

"Whoa, boy!" Josh wrapped the reins around his fist so he wouldn't let go. The big horse began to walk faster. "Whoa, boy, whoa!" Josh called.

"Hold on to that horse!" Pinkey shouted.

"I'm trying to hold him," Josh shouted helplessly.

"Stop that horse!" Pinkey aimed his rifle in the sky and shot again. The rifle cracked the air like a whip. Buddy began to bark.

"Yaaaawwwwww!! Yaaawwww!" Ben whooped out suddenly, waving his arms. The sudden noise and motion spooked the already nervous horses. Some reared up and others jumped. Then they began to run.

"Get! Get!" Ben yelled and slapped Dancing Grace on the rump. The big horse jumped forward as if he was taking off at the racetrack. The other horses stampeded straight toward Pinkey. His horse reared up, sensing the fright of the other horses.

"Go! Go!" Kim yelled, slapping her hat down on Dancing Grace's flank. The horse sped up. Josh couldn't believe how fast they were suddenly going as the horse began to gallop across the flat canyon floor. They raced east, away from the commotion behind them. Then Josh saw the split-rail fence coming up.

"Whoooooooaaaaa!" Josh yelled as the big horse approached the fence without slowing down.

"Let him run!" Kim shouted at him. She dug her boot heels into his flanks. "Let him run!"

"But there is a fence!" Josh yelled back.

Another shot ripped the air. Josh held on tighter. The big horse raced toward the fence and sped up. Just when Josh was sure they were going to go right into the fence, Dancing Grace leaped into the air. For a long moment, Josh felt like he was sailing. The sensation was terrifying and exciting at the same time. Then finally the horse hit the ground on the other side. The black thoroughbred hit the ground running.

Josh hung on for all he was worth. Kim's arms were

wrapped around his waist. Dancing Grace was moving faster. The east wall of Lost Canyon was coming up. Josh glanced over his shoulder. Pinkey was already outside the fence by the gate and was galloping after them.

"He's coming!" Josh yelled. "How do we get out of here?"

"Over there!" Kim pointed toward an opening among the boulders. Josh reined the big horse to the left. His long strides ate up the ground at a rapid pace.

"Slow down!" Josh yelled and pulled back on the reins as they reached the narrow passageway between the boulders. Dancing Grace slowed to a walk.

"Is this the right way?" Josh asked nervously as they threaded their way between two steep walls of rock that rose high above them.

"I hope so," Kim said. "Keep going. Keep going."

The big horse walked rapidly. The sound of his horseshoes hitting solid rock echoed in the narrow passageway. Finally Josh could see the opening that led to the other side. His pounding heart felt relief. The open sky ahead promised a way of escape.

Then suddenly a shadow appeared in front of them, followed by a big horse ridden by Colt Garrison. The tall cowboy looked as startled as Josh, but only for an instant. He was reaching for the rifle in his saddle when suddenly Kim shouted.

"Yaw! Yaw!" Kim yelled, digging her heels into the big horse's flanks. Dancing Grace leaped forward. Colt's horse whinnied and reared back, trying to get out of the way. Dancing Grace shot past the frightened horse, who stumbled. The tall cowboy lost his balance. He fell from the saddle and Dancing Grace leaped over him.

"Go, go!" Kim shouted, looking over her shoulder. Colt was already on his feet, trying to calm his horse. His rifle was in one hand and his reins in the other.

Dancing Grace sped up. With no canyon walls before him, he took even bigger strides. The wind raced through Josh's hair. He crouched down lower on the horse.

As the big horse ran down the main street of the ghost town, Josh felt like he was a jockey in a real horse race. The stallion ate up the ground in bounding strides. They shot through the ghost town in a matter of seconds. Dancing Grace followed the old dirt road out of town and toward the other end of the canyon.

Josh looked over his shoulder. Neither Colt nor Pinkey was in sight. The big horse kept running. They rounded a bend in the road. Up ahead, they saw the tall, chain-link fence that blocked off the front of the canyon. Josh's heart sank. The road turned. The big gate was shut.

"Whoa!" Josh yelled as they approached the gate. The horse slowed to a stop. Josh looked with dismay at the gate. A large padlock was securely in place.

"What do we do?" Josh asked anxiously. "We got a good start on Colt and Pinkey, but they'll be here soon. Colt must know we're locked in."

"Up the hill," Kim shouted, pointing to the right. "Go. Go now!"

Josh reined the big horse to the right. He started climbing up the steep hill, following the fence. Once they reached the trees, the chain-link fence became a barbed-wire fence strung between old wooden fenceposts. They climbed higher and higher, riding close to the fence.

"There!" Kim pointed ahead. Up to their left, the barbed

wire sagged between two fenceposts. One of the fenceposts leaned sideways. Kim hopped off the horse. She ran to the leaning post and kicked it with her boot. The fence post leaned farther.

"Come help me!" she said. Josh jumped down. He tied the reins to a tree branch. He ran over to help her. He kicked the fencepost with his boot. The old post leaned farther. Then they heard a shouting voice.

"Kim! Kim!" Colt's voice came up from below them through the trees. "You can't get away, Kim! Come back! No one has to get hurt."

"Harder!" Kim muttered. They kicked the post again and again. Finally Josh heard a cracking sound as the base of the post suddenly cracked. Josh stopped kicking and grabbed the top of the post. He pushed as hard as he could, leaning into the post with all his weight. He heard another crack and pop.

"We got it." Josh pushed the post down toward the ground. The barbed wires nailed to it stretched tight but flat on the ground.

"Hold the fence down while I walk him over," Kim instructed. Josh nodded.

Kim took the reins and pulled Dancing Grace toward the fence. She stepped carefully between the sharp barbed wires. She waited for the horse to pick his own steps. One of the barbs caught his back foot, and Kim stopped and waited. The horse lifted his foot and stepped again.

Down below, Josh could see a cowboy hat moving up the hill. Colt's face came into view. He grinned wickedly when he saw Josh.

"Go, go!" Josh jumped across the downed fence. But as he jumped, the barbed wire caught the bottom of his jeans. He heard a rip as he tripped forward.

"Come on!" Kim shouted. Josh yanked his leg. He felt pain and heard another ripping sound, but his leg came free. He jumped to his feet. Kim was already in the saddle. She reached down. Josh grabbed her hand. He put his foot in the stirrup and hopped up.

"You drive!" Josh said as she pulled. This time he got on behind her. She started down the hill almost before he could grab her waist. The big horse angled down the side of the hill through thick trees.

"You can't get away!" Colt yelled out behind them. "Stop or I'll shoot!"

Josh glanced over his shoulder. Colt was trying to cross the fence on horseback. But the horse stopped, his leg caught on the barbed wire.

"Go, go!" Josh yelled.

"I am," Kim said, guiding the horse through the trees. "Duck!"

Josh scrunched down, just missing a low-hanging branch. Down below they saw the road. A shot broke the air. Josh heard a bullet whiz through the air near them, cutting through the leaves on a tree. Dancing Grace rushed out into the open.

As soon as they hit the road, Kim dug her heels into the big horse. He leaped forward and began to gallop. Josh held on to Kim's waist. Once again the big horse sped down the road as if he were on a racetrack. As they started to go into a turn, Josh glanced back. Colt was just reaching the road, over three hundred yards behind them. Kim looked back too. He was leveling the rifle at them.

"Come on, Grace!" she yelled. The big horse, used to running races, galloped even faster. Up ahead Kim saw a familiar sight, her grandfather's olive-green Jeep coming down the road toward them. The old couple driving moved to the side of the road as the big black horse raced past.

"Keep going!" Josh looked back. The Jeep had turned around in the road and was following them.

"Go, go, go!" Josh yelled, seeing the Jeep speed up. "They're following us."

The Jeep sped up until it was about fifty yards behind the horse and its two riders. The road curved again and started downhill. As they raced along, the trees to their left suddenly cleared. Down below in the valley, Josh saw the welcome sight of Horseshoe Ranch.

Kim slowed the horse down. She left the road where a horse trail crossed. She guided the horse down the steep trail as fast as she could safely go. Up above them, the Jeep stopped by the trail. The old couple watched the fleeing riders.

"We can make it now!" Kim said. The trail hit the flat bottom of the valley floor. The big horse began to gallop again. He loved to run. Kim's hat blew off, but she didn't seem to notice. She guided Dancing Grace toward the entrance gate that said "Horseshoe Ranch."

Everyone in the ranch stopped to stare at the big black horse with two riders on his back. Kim's grandfather was in front of the stable. Kim raced toward him. Behind them the Jeep sped into camp just as Kim and Josh jumped off the horse. The Jeep raced up to the stables.

"Grandfather!" Kim yelled. "This is Dancing Grace, the stolen race horse! Colt and Pinkey are in on it. And so is that old couple!"

Kim pointed to the old couple who got out of the Jeep. They walked straight for Kim and Dancing Grace.

Chapter Thirteen

Grace Leads Home

Call the sheriff!" Kim said. "Colt has his rifle."

"I already did call the sheriff," Dr. Matthews said with a pleasant smile. He picked up a cell phone out of the seat of the Jeep.

"And thank you for finding Dancing Grace for us," the woman said warmly.

The old man bent down and began examining Dancing Grace's legs. He reached over and tapped on the back of his foreleg, lifting the foot and checking the shoes.

"This is Dr. Matthews," Mr. Carson said to his granddaughter and Josh. "He is a veterinarian and one of the best racehorse doctors in California."

"I was there when Dancing Grace was born," the old man said with a smile. "He looks in good shape. Hasn't even lost any weight, I'd say. And the way you were running down the road out there, he doesn't seem to have lost any of his speed either."

"A veterinarian?" Kim asked her grandfather in disbelief. Josh shrugged his shoulder and smiled. At that point he realized how rubbery his legs felt.

"I've got to sit down," Josh said. Mrs. Matthews opened the door to the Jeep. Josh gratefully sat down on the seat. The big black horse looked at him with a wet eye. Josh smiled.

By suppertime, both Colt and Pinkey had been taken into custody. The sheriff caught Colt trying to get out of the county in a stolen car. And Pinkey was caught by Ben Tucker, who lassoed him as he tried to escape out the west end of Lost Canyon.

Mr. Paloma was not from New Mexico, as he had said, but actually from Buenos Aires, Argentina. He was arrested at the ranch that afternoon by the sheriff. The sheriff found a briefcase with $500,000 in U.S. currency locked in a secret compartment in the horse trailer.

Conversation was lively that evening in the mess hall. Josh, Kim and Ben Tucker sat in the middle of all the cowhands and ranch guests, who wanted to hear the whole story. The three boys' fathers returned from their fishing trip with a cooler full of fish and lots of news to catch up on. Kim's grandfather could not stop bragging about Josh and the other boys to their dads.

"Fine sons, each one of them a real thoroughbred," Dan Carson said.

"I agree," Ben Tucker said.

"This has been a great vacation," Josh said. "I've galloped, slid down a mountain, ridden to the Continental Divide, and I even rode the fastest horse in the world."

"Mrs. Grace Adams has insisted on paying for your stay at the ranch," Dr. Matthews said. "So it's a free vacation as well.

And she has also insisted on paying the twenty-five- thousand-dollar reward to Kim and Josh."

"Twenty-five thousand dollars?" Billy murmured. "Wow! What will you do with it, Josh?"

"My dad and I already talked about that," Josh said. "We'll put most of my share of the money into a college fund. But I might get to keep some so I can take horseback-riding lessons when we get home."

"How did Mr. Paloma ever think he would get away with Dancing Grace?" Billy asked.

"He planned to take him down to the Gulf of Mexico and put him on a boat and go back to Argentina," Dr. Matthews said. "He was a wealthy man. He didn't plan to race him publicly. Even in South America people would recognize Dancing Grace. But he has many horses. He planned to breed Dancing Grace with his best mares. They would undoubtedly make very fine horses. He would have made his money back, just through breeding him."

"They also arrested Sam Bartock, the man Colt was working with at the Adams' farm," Mrs. Matthews said. "That appears to be the whole ring. I'm just glad we had time to come out here."

"It was sort of a wild-goose chase for us," Dr. Matthews said. "But I had just happened to see Colt and Sam Bartock talking together at a rodeo show a week before Dancing Grace disappeared. When I inquired and found out Colt had moved, I just wanted to check into it. There were no other leads, and even the police seemed too busy to check it out."

"So you just had a hunch?" Kim asked.

"That's right," Dr. Matthews said. "Just like young Billy had a hunch that we were up here for more than a vacation. I thought we'd be discovered for sure when you saw us go into the barn. We actually went in there to look over Paloma's truck and horse trailer. We suspected he was the buyer and had the money hidden somewhere. We figured he might have tried to hide it in the loft. Thankfully, Mr. Carson allowed us to continue our investigation when you boys turned us in for suspicious conduct."

Billy smiled sheepishly. Dr. Matthews patted him on the back.

"Were you worried Colt would recognize you?" Josh asked.

"Not too much," Dr. Matthews said. "I never had any direct dealings with him. Colt wasn't involved with the doctoring side of things back at the stables. But even if he did recognize me, I would have told him my wife and I were here on vacation, which was true, too. Whether he recognized us or not, it was a risk we just felt like we had to take."

"I liked Colt." Dan Carson hugged Kim. "But I also trusted my granddaughter's instincts. When she said she had fixed that saddle right, I began to think Colt was a liar. Pinkey confessed to me, before the sheriff took him away, that Colt thought Kim overheard their plans to sell Dancing Grace."

"So that's what it was," Kim said with a thoughtful look. "I did hear him and Pinkey whispering one day in the stable and starting to argue. They got real quiet when they saw I was there. Now that I think about it, it was after that that Colt began acting mean toward me."

"He wanted to discredit you, I suppose," Mr. Carson said. "He didn't want you around. But when he said you'd saddled Susie wrong, I began to think he was having a personality problem with you. I didn't know he was a thief to boot."

"I'm sorry I got so angry about that," Kim said. "But all his negative comments really began to hurt after a while. I felt like I couldn't do anything right around him."

Her grandfather smiled and gave her a warm hug. Kim closed her eyes as she hugged him back.

"I'm sorry he stole the horse," Kim said. "But I am glad I got to ride Dancing Grace. I can't believe I rode a horse that will probably win the Kentucky Derby. I've never ridden a horse that could run like that. He left Colt and Pinkey eating his dust."

"He's still scheduled to race," Dr. Matthews said with a smile. "We'll all be praying he wins."

"And Granddad and I will be right there with Mrs. Adams at Churchill Downs track," Kim said excitedly. "I can't wait to go."

"I promised the newspeople outside that we would go meet them and do interviews," Dan Carson said. "They're all chomping at the bit, wanting to get a story. My phone has been ringing off the hook."

Just then a wrangler poked his head in the doorway, holding up a portable phone.

"Another call, Mr. Carson," the wrangler said. He smiled and held the phone up for Mr. Carson. While the foreman of the ranch talked, the group filed outside. Several people wanted to go to the corral to look at Dancing Grace. The big horse would leave for California in the morning with Dr. Matthews and his wife.

Out at the corral, Josh watched the black stallion with admiration. The newspeople had already arrived and were taking pictures. Some of them were doing live television broadcasts. Several had requested interviews with Josh and

Kim. Some of the ranch guests took turns standing next to the famous horse while their friends took pictures. While Josh was watching all the activity, Kim rushed over.

"Guess what?" Kim asked. "My father just called! He just heard about Dancing Grace being found. Horseshoe Ranch was mentioned, and so were you and I. Granddad told him the whole story. He was really surprised. And he was really concerned about me. And you know what? He's going to come home. Can you believe it?"

"Sure I can," Josh said. "I've been praying since we talked last night up at the lodge. I didn't expect God to do it so fast, but it's kind of like the song says."

"What song?" Kim asked.

"You know," Josh replied. He began to hum the familiar tune. Kim smiled happily. Then Josh sang the last line. "'His grace has brought me safe thus far, and grace will lead me home.'"

"I think you're right," Kim said with a smile. She looked at the big horse in the corral. "Grace got us home this afternoon. And now he's bringing my father home too."

Josh and Kim were still humming as they walked over to greet the waiting people of the press.

**Don't miss the next book
in the Home School Detectives
series!**

**Here's a preview of
John Bibee's
*The Mystery of
the Widow's Watch***

Chapter Two

Herbert's Watch

W hat are we going to do?" Rebecca demanded.

"Yeah," Emily added. "Can you believe how Clarice is sticking her nose in our business like that?"

"I don't know what to do." Julie felt the anger churn inside. She was already mad about Clarice's accusations. But she had been totally shocked when she realized Mrs. Babbage assumed Clarice was part of the Home School Detectives.

Clarice looked over her shoulder and smiled very sweetly at the other three girls following behind.

"She thinks this is funny," Rebecca whispered.

Mrs. Babbage stopped and fumbled with her keys.

"Let me help you, Mrs. Babbage," Clarice offered.

"You are so polite," Mrs. Babbage said to Clarice. Clarice just smiled again. Mrs. Babbage led them inside.

"Don't you need to join the others back in the craft room?" Julie asked Clarice loudly. She stared angrily at the red-haired girl. "I know you don't want your mother to worry."

"She saw us leave with Mrs. Babbage," Clarice said.

"But this is a Home School Detective matter," Emily added flatly.

"And Mrs. Babbage wants to talk to us right away, before we help with the crafts," Clarice added with a serious voice.

"Yes, the sooner the better," Mrs. Babbage said, a fierce sparkle in her eyes. "I've been worried sick, just sick." Her eyes teared up. "It's my husband's watch."

"What about it?" Clarice asked.

"It's missing, and I absolutely must find it before . . ." The woman stopped talking as she looked off into the air.

"Before what?" Clarice asked.

"Well . . ." the old woman said uncomfortably. "Before . . . it is permanently lost. That's it. I want it back. It's very valuable to me. You will help me, won't you?"

"We will try to help you, Mrs. Babbage," Julie said.

"It's a gold pocket watch that belonged to my husband, Herbert." Mrs. Babbage rushed to the kitchenette and returned holding a small gold watch chain. "This chain used to be attached to the watch. Herbert's father gave him the watch on our wedding day. Herbert carried it all his life, even when it stopped working. The main spring was bad."

"You mean you want us to find a watch that doesn't even work?" Clarice asked. "Why not just buy a new watch?"

"The watch had great sentimental value. It must not fall into the wrong hands."

"Wrong hands?" Clarice asked with interest. "Is it some kind of spy watch? Your husband wasn't a spy, was he?"

"A spy?" Mrs. Babbage asked. "He was an accountant."

"But you said the watch shouldn't fall into wrong hands. What did you mean?" Clarice asked.

The old woman looked confused for a moment. She looked

at the floor and took a deep breath. "That was a poor choice of words," Mrs. Babbage said slowly. She turned away and looked at Julie. "Can you help me find it?"

"Do you want us to look around here?" Julie asked.

"No, no, " the old woman said. "It's not in here. That's the problem. I had it in the community room last night. I was going to have Mr. Binton put the chain back on the watch. He was a jeweler, you know. He told me he could fix it quickly."

"Mr. Binton?" Clarice asked. "Isn't he the dead guy?"

"Well. . . , yes, he expired last night of a heart attack," Mrs. Babbage said sadly. "I came back to my room to get the watch and chain after supper. But when I returned to community room, Mr. Binton's two sons and another man were talking to Mr. Binton. They've run the jewelry store since Mr. Binton retired. I sat down on the blue couch, waiting.

"Then Mr. Binton and his sons began to argue though I don't know why," Mrs. Babbage said. "Mr. Binton was an emotional man. Anyway, instead of helping me, he went back to his room with his sons without saying a word to me. I waited and waited. I really wanted my watch fixed."

"What happened next?" Julie asked Mrs. Babbage.

"Well, I was going to go back to my room when I saw Mr. Binton coming down the hallway. I smiled at him and he smiled at me. He looked very discouraged and sad. Anyway, I gave him the watch and the loose chain. He didn't say a word, and I didn't want to embarrass him. He had a little pair of needlenose pliers. He treated my watch with great care. He had just started to work when he fell over onto the floor."

"You mean he died right in front of you?" Clarice asked.

"He didn't die until two hours later," Mrs. Babbage said. "I yelled out for help, of course. Then I leaned down to see if

I could help him. He tried to whisper something in my ear. I was listening when the nurses rushed up and took over. I was quite upset, of course. He was having a heart attack."

"Wow!" Clarice said softly.

"So what happened to your watch?" Julie asked.

"It got lost once Mr. Binton fell over," the old woman said. "But I didn't realize it until later because I was upset."

"That's so sad," Julie said, nodding her head sympathetically. "Someone probably picked it up, don't you think?"

"That's precisely what I'm afraid of," Mrs. Babbage said.

"Do you think they won't return it?" Rebecca asked.

"They will know it is mine because my husband's name is on the inside cover," the old woman said wearily. "Our names and the date of our marriage date, as well as the names of our four children, are all engraved. I begged him not to do that, but he insisted. He was very proud of our children."

"If your name is in the watch, whoever finds it will probably return it," Julie offered.

"Listen, I must have my watch back, before they find it . . . ." The old woman looked at the floor. She covered her face with her hands and sobbed. The four girls watched her uncomfortably. Julie found a box of tissues and waited. When the old woman looked up, Julie handed her a tissue.

"I'm sorry," Mrs. Babbage said after she caught her breath. "This has been very upsetting for me. I did not sleep at all last night. I simply must have my watch back. Let me show you where I saw it last." The old woman quickly turned toward the door and walked out. She waited for the girls to follow and then shut the door behind them. She walked more quickly down the hall than Julie and the other girls expected.

"She's really upset about that watch," Julie whispered.

"No kidding," Rebecca replied.

"She's not telling us something," Clarice said flatly. "No one gets that worried about some old watch that doesn't even work. Something seems fishy to me about this whole thing."

"No one asked you what you thought," Emily said. "In fact, you shouldn't even be here. You aren't part of our detective team. Is she, Julie?"

"We can talk about it later," Julie said grimly. She looked sideways at Clarice. "I can't believe Mrs. Babbage can walk so fast. It does seem like she is keeping something a secret. Or maybe she is worried about something else."

The old woman walked down the hallway across the big open community room to a blue couch. "This is where we were sitting," the old woman said. "The watch is a little larger than a half dollar. It has a worn gold cover."

Julie bent down and looked under the couch. The other three girls knelt down beside her. "I don't see it under the couch," Julie said.

"Maybe someone kicked it," Rebecca said. "It would slide on this hard tile floor just like a hockey puck."

"I thought someone might have kicked it." Mrs. Babbage stood stiffly, her old gray eyes searching the floor.

"Maybe you should sit down," Julie said to the older woman. "You must be tired."

"I'll go back to my room," Mrs. Babbage said wearily. "But please bring me the watch the instant you find it."

"Yes, of course," Julie said. "We'll bring it right to you."

"Good," the old woman said. She looked at the floor once more, shook her head, turned and walked away.

"Let's spread out in four directions," Julie said.

"What about Clarice?" Rebecca asked.

"We can use all the help we can get," Julie said. "But if you find it Clarice, bring it right over to us."

"Maybe I will," Clarice said, sticking out her tongue at Rebecca. Before Rebecca could say a word, Clarice turned away, acting like she was searching the floor.

The four girls searched for thirty minutes in the big community room, looking under every couch and chair and table, almost oblivious to the activity going on around them.

"This is boring," Clarice said. "Besides, my knees are getting sore from being on this hard floor."

"We don't need your help anyway," Rebecca said.

"Well, I have another idea." Clarice then walked off.

"Where's she going?" Rebecca asked sullenly.

"Who cares?" Emily asked. "I'm glad she's gone."

"She's going down Mrs. Babbage's hall," Julie said.

"Do you think she's going back to her room?"

"She can't do that!" Rebecca said.

The three girls walked quickly after Clarice. When they hit the hallway, Clarice approached Mrs. Babbage's door.

"Let her rest, Clarice!" Julie called out.

"I have an important question," Clarice said. She was just about to knock on the door, when they heard a crashing sound inside the room. The girls froze. Julie quickly knocked.

"Mrs. Babbage, are you all right?" Julie yelled.

Clarice turned the doorknob and pushed it open. She ran inside. "Mrs. Babbage!" Clarice said loudly. Then she looked in the bedroom and screamed. The other girls rushed up beside her. Clarice's shaking arm pointed ahead of them. On the floor, they saw a pair of legs and feet with heavy dark shoes sticking out from behind the bed.

"Mrs. Babbage!" Julie cried out. Clarice screamed again.